More praise for
THE PORT OF MISSING MEN

"A sensitive chronicle of a mother-daughter relationship, a romance and a last-glimpse portrait of an age of innocence . . . Meticulously chosen metaphors and images resound throughout the novel, giving a structure and unity to this story of missing men."

San Francisco Chronicle

"Stingingly perceptive and killingly funny . . . THE PORT OF MISSING MEN is the most fun you could have with a book. Like Lily's medals, it is pure gold."

The Orlando Sentinel

"What makes it good reading is Tirone Smith's skill as a novelist, her gift for creating a world in which strange people do strange things, becoming consistently less odd in the process, until in the end we realize they aren't so different from us. . . . [This] book is a pleasure from beginning to end."

Record-Journal (Meriden, CT)

"Writing with her customary abundance of imagination, Smith spins a mesmerizing yarn that stretches from evocative scenes of Miami Beach in the 1920s to the 1936 Olympic games in Munich. The voice of Lily Neelan, a free-spirited and engagingly innocent girl, has a quirky freshness reminiscent of a character of Vonnegut."

Publishers Weekly

THE PORT OF MISSING MEN

Mary-Ann Tirone Smith

FAWCETT CREST • NEW YORK

This Book Is for Jene Maria Smith and Jere Paul Smith.
I Love You Both.

Chapter 1

My mother, Gertie Neelan, wore a hunting costume. All white—satin. Thin, slinky satin. Not transparent, but it didn't have to be. Everything showed. There was nothing under my mother's Jean Harlow dress but my mother.

The captain had been her intended quarry, but one small glimpse from her across the table told me, No, not him. Just a little bit too old. Too serious. Mostly, too busy. In a nutshell, no fun.

I wore the gold dress my mother bought for me when we were in Paris. Gold so that no one would forget who I was. I didn't like it, because every time I bent over, you could see my boobies. My mother said, "Then when you bend over, Lily, hold your dress to your chest. Modesty will endear you further to them."

Them. I was sick of *them*.

Someone approached the empty chair next to mine. I'd been wondering who might sit in that chair. While waiting for the first course, I was grateful that I only had to talk to Captain Pugnet, while the fellow who was supposed to be on the other side of me must have been too seasick for dinner. Looking back, I see how silly that was. Everyone in the world wanted to sit next to me, seasick or not. And I knew that this particular fellow, when I looked up at him, didn't know the meaning of seasickness. He was surefooted. He was a German, too, I could tell. It was the way he bowed. I thought, Uh-oh. But then he smiled. His smile was real—the kind of smile that comes easily. And he wasn't in a uniform, either. So it wouldn't be so bad sitting next to a German through a three-hour dinner, because there wouldn't be any of that Nazi laughing.

He looked at each person. There were eight of us at the captain's table, and he looked at my mother third to last. His eyes stayed on my mother a very small instant longer than on the others. Then he looked at Captain Pugnet, and the captain heaved to a stand to greet him better. Last, he looked at me. Captain Pugnet introduced us to His Excellency Mr. Albert Rexhault. His Excellency looked excellent for sure. He had missed the sail, he told us. A private yacht brought him out to meet the ship a little while ago. He was so glad that he was in time for dinner.

I said, "The ship stopped just for you?"

"Lily!"

My mother wasn't actually angry, because everyone thought my unintentionally rude remark quite adorable, and besides, it gave her a chance to let Mr. Rexhault hear her sweet, clear, excellent voice. The people smiled at me, and I looked at their sparkling white teeth and their sparkling diamonds, and then at the sparkling wall behind the banquette. The wall was polished marble, and reflected the light of the candles on the tables. The whole saloon appeared to be made of marble, and suddenly what I really wanted to do was ask the captain why the ship didn't sink. But His Excellency was talking to me, so I had to stop thinking so hard, which is what I do when embarrassed.

"It is true what you say, mademoiselle. The ship stopped just for me. I am aboard simply because I wanted to meet you. To toast your grand success. To raise a glass in salute, though you are, perhaps a bit tired of salutes."

Oh, was I ever. All I wanted was to be back in Miami Beach. On the sand in front of the Victor with Johnny Q and Eddie G. Home. But I raised my glass along with everyone else, and smiled nicely because of my mother. She was leaning forward, a little sideways in the direction of His Excellency; a lean that said, Whoa, boy, now *here's* something interesting!

His Excellency leaned right back. "That is, if madame would approve."

My mother smiled. Slyly. She had all kinds of smiles. The real kind and the kind she aimed at this fellow who had the ship pull over for him and pick him up three hundred miles off the coast of France. Fake smiling was part of my mother's job, and because she liked her job, fake smiling made her face feel good. Fake smiling made my face hurt. My mother said, "Ah'm sure there is nothin' about you, suh, of which ah might be disprovin'." Her words had that lilting kind of Southern accent, the one Europeans found especially charming. This was not her normal speaking voice. His Excellency raised his glass even higher, which meant all the men should stand, which they did.

"Then I say"—and the glasses went up higher still—"to Lily . . . among all nations . . . unequaled."

Oh, brother, can you spare me a dime? But I sipped. Champagne tastes like the juice of a sour green apple. I tried to make believe it was homemade ginger beer. Or sarsaparilla.

"And I would request the appurtenance"—The what? my eyes asked my mother. Her eyes said, Shush, Lily—"to bestow upon you"—he paused; a pause perfectly timed to allow those at the adjoining banquettes to perk up their ears—"to bestow upon you anything. Anything you wish to name. Whatever would make you happy. Your heart's fondest desire."

Sure, I thought. Then how about getting me some lemonade and heading this ship toward home, not New York? Of course, I didn't say that. I didn't know what I was supposed to say. There were oooh's and aaaah's and little nudges going on all around the table, and then everyone's eyes were all on me, all looking at me just like when I climbed the ladder to the board. The board was the only stage I was comfortable on, because I had to concentrate so hard. From the board, I was not aware of all the eyes, the upturned faces. Just my spot. My mother loved all stages, and here on the ship, it seemed she was my coach, not Eddie G, and not Mr. Marvin Modeen, either. I looked at her and then up at His Excellency Mr. Albert Rexhault, and said:

"I would like this."

Eyebrows rose. Titters tinkled around me. Only my mother's eyes narrowed, but just for a moment until she realized what I meant. Then she ran her finger along the edge of the gold-rimmed plate in front of her before raising her eyes back to me. They were filled with pride, plus a little lingering surprise.

"This?" His Excellency was intrigued, not confused.

"Yes." I gestured at the air with my champagne glass, and spilled just a few drops into my lap.

"And could you, mademoiselle, explain to me your 'this'?"

"This ship," I said. I sipped the champagne and wondered why the second sip tasted less sour than the first.

One dumb lady asked, "The *Normandie?*"

But no one really paid attention to me nodding my head yes. They thought I was masterfully amusing. The captain especially laughed. I liked him even if my mother had dismissed him. He'd worked hard to get to be captain. I understood that.

"Ah, mademoiselle," said Captain Pugnet—he had a merry voice, like Saint Nick only with a little Mr. Chevalier—"I think the French Line is, *peut-être*, not considering selling her."

Chuckles all around. His Excellency had the last word though, as he sat down in the empty chair. He whispered into my ear, "I promise you, mademoiselle, that your wish shall be granted."

I felt my mother's shoe tap my calf. I said, "Please call me Lily, Your Excellency."

"Why, I shall be charmed."

"And what should I call you?" I couldn't imagine he liked being called Excellency.

He said, "Call me Rexhault."

Now, to me, that was interesting, so I said, "Guess you don't like the name Albert, do you?"

Faux pas. But my mother figured I was due for one. She

took over. Stood straight up and asked Rexhault and the captain if she could be excused in order to powder her nose. She wrinkled her little nose like a bunny. Both men forgot me. Her timing—and I believed I learned timing from my mother, not my coaches—was faultless.

So my faux pas was forgotten. Except by a drunken duke at our table whom I liked because he reminded me of my friend back home, Johnny Q. The count was dancing with me, and we stepped all over each other's feet because I'd never learned to dance, and because he was as drunk as Johnny Q got every night before he'd finally pass out right on the beach, usually in his special hiding place between the Ritz Plaza and the Hotel Astor. The duke said:

"Such a flamboyant gesture of adoration from the kraut, Miss Lily. You are to be commended for rising so brilliantly to the occasion. The fellow's gesture of adoration, I should say, was on a par with Herod's toward Salome . . . or the Emperor Shah Jahan toward Queen whatever-her-name-was. Bully for you."

I hadn't a clue as to what he was talking about. But I could have listened to him all night because he blathered on just the way Johnny Q did, though of course Johnny Q didn't have an accent. I didn't like the way he called Rexhault a kraut though, even if all of us who'd been to the Olympic Games were glad we didn't have to look at those billions of uniforms twenty-four hours a day anymore. What I especially didn't like about the German men I'd met was that they wore uniforms all the time, always dressed like soldiers, even at parties. I asked my mother why all those fellows didn't wear suits, and she said it made them feel powerful. She said they probably slept standing up in their uniforms, so as not to make any wrinkles.

After dinner, my mother told me what the duke had meant. About John the Baptist's head and the Taj Mahal.

"Jeez," I said, "I'd sure rather have the Taj Mahal than some fella's head."

"Exactly. Which is why, Lily, I continue to tell you not to get involved in anything of a political nature."

There were two things in my life, in addition to John the

Baptist's head and the Taj Mahal story, that so far my mother had categorized as having a "political nature." The first was at home a couple of years ago in Miami Beach when I told her it was terrible that Mrs. Cloak should have a sign outside our beautiful new apartment building that said NO DOGS AND NO JEWS. Mr. Fink, who did our laundry, was a Jew. He was very old, and always gave me a licorice whip when I came to get our stuff. So I scribbled over Mrs. Cloak's sign with charcoal, and a kid squealed on me, and I got in trouble. My mother made me write a note of apology to Mrs. Cloak. And we had to pay for the new sign.

The second time was at Mr. Goebbels's private party following the formal party after the closing ceremony. Mr. Hitler was there. I told my mother, "Ya know, Ma, near as I can tell, this Mr. Hitler is a lot like Mrs. Cloak, only worse." I said that even though there wasn't any mention that Mr. Hitler hated Jews. I'd overheard two ladies discussing certain rules being developed for Jews who lived in Berlin. Then I said, "I wonder when Archie's gonna get here." Archie Williams was my friend. He won a gold medal in the four hundred meters. Archie was a real prankster, and he surely would have livened up Mr. Goebbels's boring party.

"And where's Jesse?"

My mother whisked me over behind a potted fern and told me that none of the colored athletes had been invited to the private party.

"But Jesse won *four*—"

She put her hand over my mouth. "I know that, Lily. Now, hush, and stop asking everyone why he wasn't invited. And let this be a second lesson to you. First, don't say anything with political repercussions, and second—and this is important—winning isn't everything after all."

"Not if you're colored, it isn't."

"Oh, Lily, really! That's not what I meant, and you know it!" She stalked back to the chatterboxes. I stayed with Mr. Hitler's fern plant, which would turn brown the next day. I poured a billion drinks into it.

* * *

Our second-and-a-half day on the *Normandie*, midway across the Atlantic Ocean, was the time and place my mother chose to tell me that we wouldn't be going home after all. We were going back to the United States, all right, but we weren't booked on the Silver Meteor to Miami; we were booked instead for a year of speaking engagements from Maine to California. I remained calm, assuming we'd take side trips back to Florida, like for the holidays, and then eventually go home once the tour was finished. I was most concerned with the idiocy of my giving speeches instead of diving.

"What will my speeches be about, Ma?"

"About how it feels to win two gold medals in diving at the Olympics."

"So after I say it feels great, then what will I say?"

"Don't talk smart. I'll tell you when the time comes. I will write your speeches, and you will memorize them."

"Who will I be saying your speeches to, Ma?"

"Oh . . . people like the DAR ladies and the Rotary . . . church groups . . ."

"Will they find out we don't go to church?"

"No."

"What about sports people? Will I talk to them?"

"I imagine. They'll want you to inspire youngsters to do what you've done."

I wondered how I'd pull the wool over the athletes' eyes with some speech my mother wrote.

"And then we'll go home, right, Ma?"

"Lily."

"Yes?"

"I'm afraid we have no home."

"Sure we do, Ma. The Alhambra." That was the name of the apartment building owned by Mrs. Cloak. It was white like all the other new buildings on the beach, but the trim was seafoam green, which was my favorite color trim over salmon pink and powder blue. Our foyer had a mirrored crystal ball on a pedestal, and the staircase was bordered on each side with tubes of blue neon that went from the first floor to the third, our floor. It was beautiful. I loved it. Before the Alhambra, we'd lived in a little cement-block garage that was like living in a box. I only went in the box to sleep. I even liked the rain better than that box-house.

"Listen, honey. An apartment is not a home. A house that you own is a home."

"Don't we have enough money to buy a home, then?" I was wondering if Mrs. Cloak would consider selling the Alhambra. The first thing I'd do was take down her sign. I doubted she'd sell, though. She came from Indiana to invest her inheritance. You don't sell an investment if it's where you live. My mother wasn't answering me.

"Ma?"

"Yes, we have enough money. But not enough money for the right kind of house. I don't know what we're going to do yet, Lily. Maybe at the end of the year . . ." She was growing exasperated. "For now, let's just enjoy this." She meant the *Normandie*.

"Ma?"

"Yessss, Lily." When she hissed her *s*'s, she was more than exasperated.

"What about my oak tree?"

Besides our medals, we winners had each been given an oak sapling—little German trees to be planted in every corner of the globe. My tree was stored somewhere on the *Normandie*. My mother said:

"We will donate your tree to some place that's old and scruffy and needs a tree. And someday, Lily, I promise you, you'll have a place to plant oak trees."

"Or palm trees?"

"Yes. Palm trees. But not right away."

"But I'll so miss Johnny Q and Eddie G while we're on that tour."

"I know, honey," she said. "So will I. We've been missing them for a year already. People get used to things like that. To change. You have to weigh the good against the bad."

"Home weighs more than speeches."

"It seems that way to you now, but I promise you . . . I know what I'm doing."

"Well, then . . ."

"Now let's get you to bed, Lily. It's very late."

"Are you going to bed now, Ma?"

She laughed. "You are such a little old lady sometimes. I will be having a short drink with Rexhault tonight. But I'll be careful not to wake you when I come in."

If she came in while I was still sleeping, which was doubtful. Since the Olympics had ended, we'd been guests all over Europe, and my mother would go out every night. She'd arrive back in our rooms at breakfast time, so I figured I wouldn't see her again until I was eating my cornflakes that I'd asked the porter to bring me. The French eat sandwich rolls with nothing in them for breakfast. When I asked my mother about not getting enough sleep, she told me that this was her first vacation in her life. That was true. Although I knew she was working a little. Hunting.

So that night, while my mother was having a short drink with Rexhault—why would a "short" drink take all night?— I snuck down to the pool. No one was in the pool after dinner. They were all changing from their dinner clothes to their drinking and dancing clothes. There wasn't a board at the pool, but it was a nice, quiet place. When I got there, I spotted my first famous person. The ship had lots of movie stars returning from Europe to New York, but I hadn't seen any yet. Now I saw Mr. F. Scott Fitzgerald's wife in the pool. Not that she was a movie star, but her picture was always in the papers. She winked at me. The wink meant that she knew that I knew that she wanted to be alone like me. We swam laps, and then I noticed after my half-mile lap that she was gone.

Later, I fell asleep in my bed listening to the great ship's engine hum, and dreamt about home. About Miami Beach, where my mother had worked hard every day for as long as I had known her to keep me in cornflakes while the Great Depression raged around us like a famous Florida hurricane.

Chapter 2

My mother was a prostitute. She still is, even though she doesn't turn tricks but is Rexhault's mistress. "Long term, short term—two bucks or a million . . . a hooker's a hooker," she told me. "Like being an alcoholic, Lil. Once you make your bed and get in it, you stay in it. In my case, I'm still in it even though I got out of it." She laughed at her own words. "I'm tipsy, Lil." She was tipsy a lot whenever Rexhault went away on a business trip. Who could really say for sure if maybe he'd just disappear, the way men like him tended to do. But anyway, even though a hooker was a hooker, my mother surely didn't want to go back to being the two-dollar kind.

When I was four years old, my mother reclaimed me at her mother's house in New Haven. She'd decided to try her luck in the "boomingest" town in the United States. The Billion-Dollar Sandbar. The New Paradise on Earth. The Modern-Day Tahiti. The name that was on everyone's lips. Miami Beach. Trouble was, two days before she boarded the train, Florida was ripped up by the worst hurricane of all time. That was in 1926, but she went off anyway with the little girl she wasn't able to leave behind, figuring to make hay with all those game people who intended to rebuild the resort to what it had been before the monstrous storm. She'd give it a whirl. Well, on the train, my mother got in with all these architects and builders who showed her their plans for sea-washed, pastel-colored homes and hotels and movie theaters trimmed with sunbursts and flamingos and porthole windows. She was enchanted. There were no pastel colors or flamingos in New Haven.

She meant to take my granny, too, but told me Granny refused to leave her cats. The Cat Woman of Whitney Avenue, she was called.

"A perfect granny was your granny, Lil. Treated you like one of her cats. Petted you all day, and gave you treats, and let you destroy her house." My mother laughed. "Of course, she was mad as a hatter, but everyone knows kids are really crazy people. You had a wonderful childhood with your granny, that's for sure."

"Why did you bring me with you, Ma? You couldn't have loved me. You hardly even knew me."

" 'Course I loved you, Lily. But more important, I owed you. I had you, so I owed you. About that time, I knew your granny would never send you to school. After all, you don't send cats to school. So I couldn't let you grow up thinkin' you were Puss in Boots, now could I?"

I remember, just barely, arriving in Miami. I thought I was in a fairy story. In New Haven, the summer had ended, and now it was back. That was magic to me. I remember how warm the sun was on my bare arms. What I don't remember was the devastation of the hurricane that my mother later described to me. She said the hurricane had been so bad that all the tropical birds Mr. Pancoast had imported to fill his seaside gardens had been blown over to the mainland. They never came back, either. The mainland of Florida didn't have a single cockatoo or flamingo or parrot until the hurricane ripped up Miami Beach. At first, my mother was afraid the birds were trying to tell her something, but—as she put it later—"Damned birds were wrong!"

The first thing my mother did was move us into the concrete box that had been a fellow's garage that he'd converted into living quarters for his first hooker. His first hooker felt the same way as the birds. She wasn't about to chance another hurricane. She left, and my mother moved in. I think I remember that hooker, because the second thing I can remember about my first few days in Miami Beach—after the sun on my arms—was a lady with a ring made out of a gold nugget. I remember the gold nugget on her finger because that's what I stared at when she gave me a little bottle of perfume. I was a shy girl then. Except with cats. My mother told me I'd hold a gabfest with every cat I'd run into, and holy mackeral if the cats didn't act like they knew exactly what I was talking about!

The second thing my mother did was to secure an appropriate baby-sitter for me. Johnny Q. She gave it to him for free when he agreed to watch me and not be drunk while I was in his charge. He took care of me from 7:00 A.M. until 5:00 P.M., and then drank all night.

Inside of a week, my mother developed eight groups of clients, mostly the architects and builders she'd met on the train. She referred to the groups as the "on-their-way-to-work fellas"; the "late-for-work fellas"; the "coffee-break fellas"; the "early-lunch fellas"; the "lunchtime fellas"; the "late-lunch fellas"; the "leave-work-early fellas"; and the "on-their-way-home-from-work fellas." Eight tricks a day with just enough space between the "lunchtime fellas" and the "late-lunch fellas" for her own lunch, which she had with me and Johnny Q.

Some nights, after she'd tuck me in, she'd tell me she was going to visit with the man in the house who let us use his garage. She'd lock me in, but I wouldn't fall asleep until she came back. When you're four, you know when something isn't right even when you can't figure out exactly what it is.

My mother was young, clean, well-dressed, and very pretty. She had beautiful legs. Her clients gave her two dollars each. Eighty dollars a week was big money in Miami Beach in the late twenties, and even bigger money during the Depression. Because of the Depression, my mother never got a raise as the years went on, but she was grateful for what she had. Once I heard her tell Johnny Q, "We're poor here in Miami Beach, but most people in the country are a hell of a lot worse off. I can't think what would have become of me if I'd stayed up North. Now, we got sunshine and coconuts. No matter what, we got our sunshine and coconuts, and I'm surely glad of that."

As soon as the Alhambra was finished, we moved in. Mr. Fraley was the man who'd built and owned the Alhambra before he sold it to Mrs. Cloak. Once a week he came and spent a few hours with my mother in her bedroom. It wasn't like the garage at all. My mother and I each had our own room to sleep in, and there was also a kitchen and a sitting room. My bedroom was the balcony, which Mr. Fraley had glassed in for me. I like Mr. Fraley. I hated the garage man.

The Alhambra was one of the buildings designed by my mother's clients who gave the world tropical deco. The last thing the architect of the Alhambra did was to carve into the stucco arch over our doorway a row of hieroglyphics. He copied them from a magazine picture of King Tut's tomb that everyone was talking about. All the corners of the Alhambra were curved, and he wanted to "enhance the curves with one last special touch, Lily." I sat by his feet and held up the picture of the tomb while he copied the hieroglyphics.

When I started school, my mother told me to tell all the kids—if they asked—that she was a widow. They asked. So, I thought a widow was a lady who went to work every day the way men did. My mother did her work as far as possible from South Beach, where we lived. She protected me from finding out what she was doing.

At school, the gang would say:

"My pop's a painter."

Or, "My pop's a mason."

Or, "My pop's a steam fitter."

I'd say, "I don't have a pop, but my ma is a widow."

But then, when the girl who sat next to me in school said her mother was a war widow, I knew I didn't have things quite worked out. Johnny Q decided to tell me the real story. Not quite the real story, as it turned out. Johnny Q was the only person I ever really talked to. My mother and I discussed things like which movie we'd go see on Saturday night, or which was better—a strawberry or a chocolate soda. Happy things. First Johnny Q told me what a widow really was, and then he told me what my mother really was. But I didn't see anything wrong or unusual about his description of how my mother spent her working hours. Selling herself to be played with for twenty minutes—"played with" was how Johnny Q expressed sex. I figured he meant she played poker with them or tennis, and all the other things adults played at on Miami Beach. Selling playtime to men was, to me, like selling shoes, only more fun. Johnny Q explained that if kids knew what she did, they'd be mean to me and make fun. Eventually, they did find out, but I didn't care what they said, because by then, as my mother put it, we were "on our way!" I've heard since that daughters of prostitutes are more innocent than daughters of reverends.

The reason we were "on our way" was because of Johnny Q. "Who'd have thought it?" said my mother at least once a week. Johnny Q was a down-and-out athlete. He played professional baseball for fifteen years. He played for the Chicago White Sox, who later became more well known by their moniker—the Black Sox. My mother told me not to talk to him about being a famous baseball player. I did, though, a few years later. All my mother said was that he was kicked out of baseball and put on trial. I thought that baseball must surely have been a tough game. If you stunk, you got arrested. My mother said that after the trial, his wife had left him, took his kids—where, he didn't know—sold their house and everything in it, and threw away what was left. So Johnny Q had nothing—no family, no place to live, and no earthly possessions. Not even the autographed baseball with the names of all his old teammates when he'd pitched his no-hitter.

"Did he go to jail, Ma?"

"He was cleared."

"What's cleared?"

"Lily, the damn fools had no proof against Johnny Q. And there was a big load of what they call extenuatin' circumstances. He never threw any game!"

"Threw a game? What's that?"

"Take money to lose."

I was shocked. I wasn't competing yet at that point, but

I knew I would be soon, and I wouldn't take a million dollars to lose. Neither would Johnny Q have done such a thing, for sure. Anyway, that was why Johnny Q ended up a drunk in Miami Beach. Because the Commissioner of Baseball wouldn't let him play ever again.

Fortunately, he was a handy guy, so the first hotel to go up after the storm—the Cardoza—hired him to be their Mr. Fix-it. He could fix anything. I tagged along behind him through the hotel corridors while he fiddled with wires or took a wrench to the pipes. Right away he taught me to swim, so that when I was bored I could go in the hotel pool. Not in the ocean, because I was only four years old. He figured I wouldn't drown in the pool what with all the people around. The pool was where I was happiest. I was an excellent swimmer, with a healthy fear of water. I especially loved jumping in from the side.

My second-favorite thing, growing up on the beach, was having a catch every day with Johnny Q. When I had my fifth birthday, he bought me a mitt. We'd go to Mr. Pancoast's park, and Johnny Q would teach me how to throw a blooper and a fastball, a sinker and a knuckler and a spitter. I was one of those kids who was never sure which hand to write with, left or right, so Johnny Q tried to help by getting me a left-hander's mitt, too. I'd throw right-handed until I felt uneven, and then I became a south-paw. Back and forth, back and forth. He said a person should just do what comes naturally. So some days I pitched to him righty, and sometimes lefty. My mitts were my favorite toys. I'd keep them oiled and neat, and that made Johnny Q very happy.

I got to know all the people rebuilding the beach. My favorite guy was the Putty Man. He was colored, and that was the name everyone called him. They still do. He came around in a rusty truck with tubs of putty he'd mixed himself. His first job outside the colored folks' neighborhood was replacing the broken windows from the hurricane. Then he got hired by the Northerners to put in the windows of their tropical-deco construction. Once a week he'd come to the end of Fifteenth Street to the Cardoza, which was near our Alhambra. He'd give me a lump of putty to play with.

When he was done with his jobs in the neighborhood, I'd beg him to make things for me. What he could do with that putty! He'd make me birds and nests with baby birds in the nests, and pine trees and little houses, and I'd bring them home and put them on my shelf to dry.

When builders began to see how talented the Putty Man was, they gave in to a request he'd made. The contractors let him paint great big murals on the empty stucco interior walls of their beautiful buildings. In the mid-thirties, when a hundred buildings a year were put up, the Putty Man would try to finish up his work so he could get in some painting time. Johnny Q would let me go with him to watch if he wasn't working too far away. The Putty Man would give me a little brush and some paint and let me paint pictures on big strips of cardboard he'd find for me.

The Putty Man was never paid a dime for that work, and no one today knows who did the paintings. I do. But the Putty Man told me that he didn't want anyone to know he did them, because the paintings weren't all that good. They were. Johnny Q told me the real reason. The Putty Man was a true artist. Never satisfied. Just like me. No matter how well I was diving. I was always sure I could be better. The only reason the Germans handed me two gold medals was not because I was the best in the world, but because I happened to be just a little bit better than the other girls who were there to compete at that particular time.

About a year after my mother and I came to Miami Beach, Johnny Q ran into an old friend from his amateur days, back before he played for the White Sox. Eddie G. Eddie G, Johnny Q told me, almost made it to the Olympics himself as a diver. But he didn't have any backing. He tried baseball for a while, but in the end became a swimming and diving coach. Then things went sour for him up in New York, so he came down here. For such a long time, I never knew that a particular class of people went by their first names plus a letter. I thought Que and Gee were their last names. My mother explained to me that they were missing men with no place to go. She said only if you're rich like Rexhault could a missing man use his real name. Money, my mother said, was more than stuff you spend on nail polish. It was also protection, like an invisible guard dog.

Eddie G was a swim pro at the Miami Beach Bath Club. When the two men met up, they hugged and then they sat under a palm tree and talked while I hid behind Johnny Q's back. After Eddie G offered Johnny Q the job, Johnny Q said:

"I can't lay off the sauce, Eddie."

"Have you tried?"

"No."

"Why not?"

"Because I like it. But I only drink at night. I want you to know that. If you give me the work, I'll be sober as a judge. Want you to know that."

"You're a man of your word, Johnny."

"Thanks." Johnny Q looked down.

Eddie G said, "But about the kid. Is he . . . ?"

"She. She ain't mine." I made sure Johnny Q's back hid me completely.

"So whose is she?"

"Belongs to a friend. I take care of her during the day. Her mother turns tricks. We got a deal. But the kid won't get in the way. I promise you that. She's a real good little kid. No trouble." I peeked up over Johnny Q's shoulder.

"You say it's a girl?"

"Yeah." My hair was in a short bob, and all I had on was a boy's bathing trunks. "C'mon around here, Lily, and say hello to my friend Eddie G."

I edged out. Eddie G reached over and ruffled my hair. "Good name for this kid."

"Yeah." My hair was short, but it was thick and straight, bleached from blond to white by the sun.

"Pretty kid."

"Yeah."

I came around till I was standing a little to the side of Johnny Q, leaning carefully into his shoulder.

"Lily, huh?"

"Yeah. Lily."

"Built to dive."

Johnny Q smiled at him, then at me. He put his arm around my shoulders and gave me a little squeeze, "Ain't that the truth."

Built to dive. I surely was. I had long, narrow muscles. My shoulders were wide, my hips compact, and my legs tapered down to small, strong feet. As I grew up, I had no visible body fat except for my round rear. Two grapefruit, my mother said. When I got breasts, my mother said two grapefruit in the back and two oranges in the front.

Eddie G and I were a perfect partnership. Not only was he a great sports coach, he had an artistic eye, which is important with diving, since it is as much theater as it is sport. He had me grow my hair long. Then he pulled it back very tight—too tight—and made a thick braid. His granny had been an Indian. She'd taught him to do that to her hair. With oil, he patted any wisps straight back from my forehead.

"Smooth as an arrow," he'd say. He'd say it a lot, so I wouldn't forget that that's what I was trying to look like, and one day he even shot an arrow into the water. I wasn't diving that day, because I had a little cold.

"Any splash, Lily?"

"No."

"That's how you enter the water every time. Just like the arrow that you are." Then he handed me a Kleenex for my runny nose. "Someday you might be up there going for a big prize, Lily, and you might have a cold like you do today. Might have influenza. Now you can feel sick before you step up on the board and after you get out of the water, too, but you can't be sick when you dive. Okay? Bad luck is part of sports. It'll be bad luck to have a cold when you're trying to win a prize, so you have to drive bad luck out with your will."

"Okay." Made sense to me. I blew my nose, made believe I had no cold, made believe I didn't feel blue, and dived all day. But with a lot of rest periods, and Eddie G kept having me suck on oranges.

I practiced day after day, week after week, trying to dive like an arrow. Every time I entered the water and made more splash than Eddie G allowed for, I'd have to repeat that dive ten times. And if in that ten times I created splash—ten more dives for each. He was tough. So was I. I never stopped until he told me. When I was really little, I'd beg him to teach me some new stuff all the time, and he had to explain that the coach makes all the decisions, the athlete none.

After I'd been diving two years, when I was six, I had to learn what was the hardest thing of all—to dive in a girl's bathing suit. Until then, I dived in my little trunks. It was tough learning to dive in a long wool tunic and knee-length breeches. I hated it. My mother said:

"Get used to it, Lily. Can't let a little thing like that get in your way."

Johnny Q told me why she was so harsh. "Your ma wants you to end up on Easy Street, Lily. Only way to get there is to be tough."

"And will you be on Easy Street with us, Johnny Q?" I thought we were talking about a particular place.

"Nope. I been there. I don't know how to live on it. See, Lily, once you've been on Easy Street, you begin to feel a new power. Like you can do anything. Like nothing can go wrong. But it ain't so. Now, when you get on Easy Street, Lily, you remember what it was like before. Be grateful for whatever you get, or you'll lose it."

"But I'll miss you when I'm on Easy Street."

He laughed. "No, you won't, kid. 'Cuz I'll still love ya even when it's time for me and you to split up."

"Well, then, I ain't goin' to no Easy Street." I stomped off, hurt. All alone, I cried about splitting up with Johnny Q and wearing that damned bathing suit. But the Roaring Twenties had been roaring in, and suddenly everyone stopped wearing those bathing costumes, and wore skimpy little numbers that made you look more naked than when you were naked. And I forgot about Easy Street. For the time being.

"To become a champion, Lily, to be perfect, you must be just like this." It was my birthday. Eddie G handed me a mechanical doll. It was a walking Casey the Cop doll. I was too old for a doll, not that I ever much cared for them, but Eddie G had something important to teach me. He wound up Casey, and put him down. The doll walked straight across the deck of the pool, one foot in front of the other, as if he were marching in the Arbor Day parade.

"That's precision, Lily," Eddie G said. "Now watch this."

He wound him up again, and stood him six inches from the bathhouse wall. He let Casey go.

"So what happens when he hits the wall, Lily?"

"He keeps walkin'."

"That's right. Does he fall?"

"Nope."

"Keep watchin'."

When Casey's machinery ran down, he fell over.

"See. He fell down when he stopped. Don't you stop ever, Lily. Don't even let solid walls stop you."

"I won't, Eddie G."

"There'll be a lot of them."

"I won't stop."

We shook hands. Johnny Q was watching this whole performance nearby. He kicked a rock.

A hundred dives a day. That became the regimen. At a hundred dives a day, my head felt split open by midafternoon. But I kept diving until my skull could adapt to the pounding. My mother heard me crying out on my balcony one night, before my skull had finally adapted. She came out in her beautiful peignoir that floated all around my cot as she sat down on the edge. "What is it, honey-girl?" I told her I wished my head would stop making such a racket just long enough for me to fall asleep. So she held the back of my head with one hand and pressed her other hand against my forehead, and pushed. That felt very good. Because of my bad headaches, my mother insisted on getting into the act. She called a meeting after work the next day.

Johnny Q and Eddie G waited with me in our sitting room while my mother took her bath, which she always did when she came home from work. She came out in her Chinese robe, drying her crimped hair with a big Turkish towel. She sat right between Johnny Q and Eddie G on the sofa, stuck a cigarette in her holder, put her feet up on the coffee table, and waited while my baby-sitter and my coach finally figured out to pick up the round marble table lighter and light her up.

"Okay, fellas," she said, "what's the plan here?" Johnny Q was already in his cups—he was swigging from his bottle the whole time my mother was in the bathtub—so he started talking while Eddie G was still working up his courage. Eddie G was a little afraid of my mother.

"Ya see, Gert," said Johnny Q, "our Lily is a natural athlete. She just needs special trainin'. And Eddie G here is the best there is, and he's just doin' what he hasta do."

"The best what? I thought you fellas were baseball players."

"A professional athlete can do anything, Gert. Eddie G lived near the water as a kid, so he started out a swimmer and diver. He tried a little baseball and was damn good, but he wasn't a team man. But right now he could go one-on-one on the court with any amateur basketball player and beat all shit outa him."

Eddie G cleared his throat. He acted one way around men and another way around ladies. For example, he didn't swear in front of a lady, even if she was a hooker.

"But where is this special trainin' you're always talkin' about gonna get her? I mean besides a helluva headache." My mother had her eye locked right into Eddie G's. She didn't want any B.S. creeping in.

Eddie G said, very softly, "Berlin."

"Beg pardon?"

"Berlin. In Europe."

"Yeah, I know where it is."

Johnny Q said, "Berlin in '36."

"We're talkin' about 1936?"

"Yeah."

"So what's happening there in 1936?"

"The Olympics, Ma," I said. I sidled over to her chair. I was ten years old; Berlin in 1936 seemed a long ways away. If it mystified me, what was it doing to my mother?

My mother threw her head back and roared with laughter. She laughed and laughed. She poured herself a glass out of

Johnny Q's bottle. She dumped it down her throat. Finally, she said, "Why, you coupla old has-beens. I thought I had some crazy ideas for my little gal here. School. College. I mean, she's a smart kid. But you guys are talkin' Sonja Henie here. You're talkin' Babe Didrickson. You're talkin' B.S.!"

Johnny Q poured my mother another drink. No one spoke for what I figured was a real long time, so I said, "We're gonna do it, Ma."

Now, she just sipped at her whiskey. She looked at Johnny Q, then at Eddie G, and then she looked at me.

"Lily, I wanna watch ya dive."

"Okay, Ma."

"Now."

"It's night, Ma."

"I can see that, kiddo. Eddie G, your pool got lights?"

"Yes, ma'am."

My mother mumbled "ma'am" under her breath, laughed again, and led the way to the bath club.

I did an inward pike with a full twist. The hardest dive I could do perfectly. If you weren't a diver, you called it a back jackknife where the guy turns around in midair. The people who were strolling around clapped for me.

When I climbed out of the pool, my mother's eyes were narrow. She beckoned to me with one long finger with its long, long red fingernail. I came over and stood next to her, dripping.

"Lily, I don't know anything about diving. This guy"—she hooked a thumb at Eddie G—"obviously knows plenty. But what I *do* know plenty about is entrances and exits. Lily, when you climb out of the pool, don't haul yourself out like some kind of drowned mule. Spring out, same way you sprung in. And smile. And . . . and . . . how old will you be in '38?"

"Thirty-six, ma'am," said Eddie G.

"Thirty-six, then."

"I'll be fifteen, Ma."

"Fifteen . . . Well, then, Lily, you practice smiling while you're climbin' out of the pool and . . . and make sure to stick out your chest!"

Chapter 3

The captain took Rexhault and me on a tour of the *Normandie*. We met with him at 6:00 A.M. in a part of the ship that was below the waterline where there were no portholes to ever let light in. The men down there had yellow skin the same color as the waxy light. All the other passengers were asleep. At least I never saw any as we went down and down long, winding stairs. I'd gotten my eight hours, and I figured that Rexhault—between the time he left my mother and called on me—had time to shower and change, but not sleep, and he looked exactly as bushy-tailed as he was two nights before when he told me he'd give me the *Normandie*. I didn't bring that up, though I was tempted to tease Rexhault about it. But Captain Pugnet didn't think much of flamboyant gestures of adoration when they concerned his ship. He was very serious about his ship.

He didn't give us a tourist tour, either. Rexhault wanted to see exactly how the ship was put together. So what if the tour might get boring, I didn't care. I was just dying to do something besides eat and swim in the indoor pool, which was actually quite a spooky place. I only saw Mrs. Fitzgerald that one time. She must have thought it was spooky, too. The indoor pool was done totally in an aquamarine tile frieze, with lights shining everywhere so you'd think you were outside. A brochure I'd read said that the pool gave off the glow of a balmy day. It didn't. And most people didn't swim anyway unless they'd spent a few too many

23

hours at the adjoining bar, which was gilded bronze. Swimming with drunks is dangerous. They think that you're a buoy someone threw in for them to lean on.

And there was no board. Not at the outdoor pool, either, where it was too cold to swim. My mother said:

"That's okay, Lily. I know you're aching to go jumping off some plank of wood, but from now on, people will have to pay to see you dive. You'll just have to wait till we're back in New York. It's a sacrifice, but as you get older, you'll find that life's full of sacrifices."

"This is a big one, Ma."

"I know it is, honey. But now you have a chance to just sit back and look over what the world is really about. What's out there for you. Like a ballerina who broke her foot or a diva with tonsilitis."

"But what about the next Olympics? Mr. Modeen said . . ."

"First off, with all those European countries at each other's throats, I don't imagine we're going to see another Olympics for a while. But, Lily, once is plenty. Time to move on. Time for the two of us to quit workin', and for Mr. Modeen to find himself a new star."

"Mr. Modeen's going to be mad."

"He was."

"Oh."

"But now he's not. He's getting a big chunk of your tour money. And he also realized that getting a new star would be real easy. You've built him some reputation."

She didn't even asked me how I felt about not training anymore, and I didn't know how I felt, either, though diving with Mr. Modeen was not the fun it had been with Eddie G. I liked to please Eddie G. Mr. Modeen never showed his pleasure. In the weeks following the Olympics, I actually thought it was nice to watch the world from someplace other than a ladder. And there was so much of the world. I had a lot to tell Johnny Q and Eddie G when I got back. That is, after I finished telling them what happened during every single minute of the Olympic Games.

Captain Pugnet's tour started with the keel plates. We saw

tons and tons of chunks of steel that the ship was made of. And while the captain pointed out the bulkheads and wave breaks and upper hulls and new gravity davits, his words seemed to me to have nothing whatsoever to do with the mammoth pieces of metal he would knock on with his knuckles.

"The *Normandie*," he told us, "is the first liner to be built without a straight bow. Our architect experimented bravely and gave the world something more graceful than could be imagined. A liner with a beautiful, clipper-ship bow. Such sleek lines. Such curving serenity."

Rexhault said, "Surely, the clipper design serves more than beauty."

I grew more and more interested. There were a lot of clipper ships that came to Miami Beach, and they were very beautiful, I thought.

"Ah, *mais oui*! We can do the same speed as the *Queen Mary* and use one-fifth less horsepower."

"And fuel?"

"Far less fuel, monsieur!"

Rexhault's voice grew deeper. "And perhaps considering what lies ahead, this is an important feature."

"If you mean war," the captain said, "I refuse to think about the future of my ship. The *Normandie* would, of course, be confiscated. All the great liners will be confiscated and refitted as troop ships." Captain Pugnet's face became grave. I wished I could cheer him up, but he and Rexhault got into war talk. I let them for a while and didn't pay attention. I should have. Maybe then I would have been better prepared for a few years down the road when I saw how the U.S. Army had also confiscated all the hotels on Miami Beach and refitted them, too. Instead, I interrupted the conversation. I asked, "How'd they get that *Normandie* sign up there at the top of the ship?"

They stared at me, having forgotten that I was still hanging around, and they both smiled. They smiled at their forgetting all about me. Captain Pugnet promised me that at the end of the tour we would go up to the dog promenade, where I would be close enough to the letters to touch them.

The dog promenade was part of the upper sundeck surrounding the stacks. The sign hung aft, between the second and third stacks, but the captain told me that the French Line was thinking of removing it because some considered it garish for such a beautiful lady. (My mother would have called that B.S., and Captain Pugnet would have agreed with her.)

The sign was made of hundreds of electric light bulbs spelling out the name THE NORMANDIE. At night, the letters seemed suspended in midair. The sign reminded me of Miami Beach, just as it had a year ago in New York when I'd first seen it. It was a lovely sign, even turned off. And I reached up and touched one of the bulbs.

Besides the sign, what was also quite interesting way up there, was that the third stack was actually a fake; it was there only for aesthetic balance. I told the captain that I understood all about balance. He said, "You do, you do!"

And I met a couple of nice pooches up on the promenade getting walked by stewards.

"I like dogs, Captain Pugnet. We couldn't have them at my apartment building."

The captain huffed and said, "All dogs, as well as children, should live in the country, not in apartments."

Rexhault said, "But captain, Lily would not have learned to dive in the country."

The captain looked at me, rather sadly I thought, and said, "Ah, I forget what a special child we have here with us." He patted my head just the way I patted the dogs' heads—with pity and affection.

I was just about to bring up that no Jews were allowed at the Alhambra, either, but instead I took my mother's advice about not getting into anything political, though it was hard to keep still. I wanted to ask why people were so cruel to each other. Like the people who had been so cruel to Johnny Q. The captain and Rexhault, I was sure, could answer any question I asked, but it was finally time for the captain to get back to steering his ship. Rexhault and I went to breakfast.

The breakfast salon smelled so good. Even though those

French rolls taste like nothing, they smell like the be-all and the end-all while they're cooking.

Soon my mouth was full of cornflakes, along with bites of deep-fried dough with sprinkled cinnamon that the waiter brought me. I could tell he didn't believe those little thin pieces of crunch I'd ordered could possibly fill a person up, which was exactly how I felt about his silly rolls. But I didn't say anything to him. I was afraid that might be political.

While I ate, Rexhault drank coffee and stared at me. I stared back. So he said:

"Lily, how are you adjusting to this life? A life without diving."

I chewed and swallowed. "Well, I feel like I've left that part of me somewhere—like on a shelf somewhere—and as soon as I get back to Miami Beach, I'll take it down."

"You won't miss the competition? Your mother says you will no longer compete."

"Well . . . Eddie G taught me—"

"Eddie G?"

"Yes. My first coach in Miami Beach. Florida."

"Ah . . ."

"He taught me to compete against myself, not the other divers. I always try to do better than the time before. I always tried to do my best, and when I did my best, the next time I'd try to dive a better best."

I took a big drink of pineapple juice. He smiled. "I know what you mean."

"Good. Lots of people don't."

"I believe your mother knows, too."

"Yes. She does."

"You have a year of speaking engagements lined up. Then what?"

"Good question."

"What does you mother tell you?"

"Nothing. But one thing I know."

"What's that?"

"She's sick and tired of being a hooker."

He dropped his spoon into his coffee cup, and a few drops

sloshed out. "Lily! If you must be so blunt, at least keep your voice down!"

"Sorry."

I started eating some strips of bacon I found under a silver bowl near the coffeepot. Rexhault didn't say anything for quite a while. Didn't eat, either. So I finally whispered, "A man like you must have been able to tell my ma's a hooker. After all, you didn't bring her back this morning till five A.M."

He sighed. "There are different sorts of . . . ah . . . as you say, hookers."

"Really?"

"Oh, yes. There are the very poor kind, who have no means to survive except to sell themselves. And—"

"That's the kind my mother was back in Bridgeport. My granny had to take care of me then. In New Haven. That's near Bridgeport. Both those places are in Connecticut, Rexhault. Have you ever been to Connecticut?"

"Well, as a matter of fact, I have."

"Is it nice?"

"Very lovely."

"I don't remember it much."

His eyes shut, then opened. "Shall we get back to what we were discussing?"

I would have said no, but my mouth was full again, and Rexhault didn't notice me shake my head. He said, "At the other end of the scale, Lily, there are the kind of . . . hookers . . . who are beautiful and exciting and are taken care of by just one man."

"That's getting married, Rexhault."

"Not quite. That's being a mistress."

"My mother's been that."

"Has she?"

"Sure. When we came to Miami Beach, my mother was a guy's mistress so we could live in his garage. I mean, not a real garage. My ma made it as nice a place as she could. She—"

"Lily . . ."

"And don't forget, if you're a lady who takes care of a dog, you're also called a mistress."

He laughed. A real laugh, loud.

"Rexhault?"

"Yes, Lily?"

"Are you lookin' to have my mother be your mistress?"

"I believe so."

"Why not a wife?"

"A wife wouldn't like me. But, Lily, don't tell your mother that I'd like her to be my mistress."

As if my mother didn't know that.

"What would you think of that, Lily? Living with me as well as your mother?"

I looked at him. His thick dark hair. His ascot. His golden-brown eyes. He had a dimple in his chin. A deep one, like Johnny Q's. "I'd like that. You remind me a lot of my friend Johnny Q."

"And who is this Johnny Q? Another coach?"

"Nope. He's a drunk."

He laughed again. I could have said that my mother was sort of Johnny Q's mistress, too, but that would have been mean.

"You're so funny, Lily. Your mother is, too. Cynical humor and the humor of an innocent—together, the two of you are simply quite wonderful. I like women who make me laugh."

"Me, too. And men."

"Your Johnny Q would make you laugh?"

"Oh, yes, all the time."

He put his chin in his hand and said to me, "But I haven't made you laugh, have I?"

"Nope."

"Well, then, I hope I will be able to change that."

I wiped bacon grease off my fingers with the big white napkin that the waiter had spread across my lap. I looked across the table into the nice eyes of His Excellency Albert Rexhault. I said:

"So tell a joke."

Chapter 4

When I was ten, Eddie G brought out the portable platform for me. I could only use the platform from 5:00 to 7:00 A.M., before the first club members wandered out to the pool. Before me, the platform was only used during diving exhibitions, and usually the diver was dressed as a clown and did a lot of silly free-falls. I even heard that one clown was actually a parachutist who learned how to hit the water without killing himself. Eddie G never told me when I could try the platform for the first time, because then I would have anticipated it. He wanted my mind clear of everything but the business at hand. Whenever I asked him about trying the platform, he'd always say, ''Not for a long time.'' Johnny Q kept the platform, all assembled, out of sight in the middle of a circle of palms. When Johnny Q wheeled it out for the exhibitions, I was forbidden to go near it. That was frustrating for me. I wanted badly to dive from it.

I tried not to think about it and to remind myself that I had to concentrate on the springboard and stop pining for something I couldn't have. My mother told me everybody's got to have dreams, and I should be grateful I had something to dream about getting someday I'd actually get. She said the dreams she had as a child were impossible ones. She knew what she was talking about, because one day that was no different from all the others, I got to the club and there was the platform, waiting for me. The time had arrived for my dream to come true. Johnny Q in his role as baby-sitter had to hold on to me to keep me from scrambling up the ladder.

"Before you go up, Lil," Johnny Q said to me, "you pay real close attention to what your coach has to say."

Eddie G, it turned out, insisted on giving me a long lecture about springboard diving and platform diving being two different sports, and how there was a good chance I wouldn't be as good off the platform.

"I will be, Eddie G," I told him.

"Now, Lily, I ain't lettin' you up there till you listen to me. So shake the ants outa your pants, first off. I want you to take a good, hard, long look at that platform."

I looked up. I was so itching to climb up that ladder, I could feel the rungs pressing into the balls of my feet. The balls of my feet were what were itching the most. I looked at the platform itself, and then down in a straight line to the water. How much more I could do in that grand amount of space! I saw myself twisting, rotating, reversing into somersaults. I could hardly hear what Eddie G was saying. I tried to listen, though, because he was my coach. A kid who's an athlete can get away with not listening to his mother and not listening to his schoolteacher, but he can't miss a single word from his coach.

"It's dangerous, Lily."

"Goddamned dangerous," Johnny Q said from behind Eddie G's shoulder. Eddie G gave him a look.

"Hit your head on the platform, you're dead before you reach the water."

Johnny Q piped up again. "Old Eddie's seen a man leave the back quarter of his skull up on the platform, right, Eddie G?"

Eddie G bent down to me so we were eye-to-eye. "You listening, Lily?"

"Yes. So now can I go up?"

Eddie G took me by my shoulders, still eye-to-eye. "You ain't climbin' that ladder till I know you're hearin' me."

"I'm hearin' you, Eddie G."

He took a real big breath. He looked up at his hand grip-

ping my shoulder. Very softly, he said, ''I saw a kid break
his neck first time off the platform.'' He suddenly stood up.
Johnny Q butted in:

''That there was different, and it was a long time ago.
That ain't gonna happen to Lily. She's been coached good.''

I said, ''Wow, how'd the kid break his neck?''

Eddie G was pacing a little while I was saying that, but
then he stopped right in his tracks. He came up to me and
planted his feet in front of mine. He said in a grievous
voice, ''Lily, once you get in the air and you're not prepared, and you hit the water bent, your neck will break. Or
your back. Any kid up there . . . any adult up there the first
time gets plenty scared. You're gonna be scared, too, Lily.
You might have to climb up and down that ladder all day, all
week maybe, before you get the gumption to jump off.
Maybe there won't be that much gumption in you. And if
not, that's all right. That's all right. We're talkin' two different sports here, and there's no need to be good at both.''

''I'll have the gumption,'' I said. God, how I wanted to
dive from that platform!

Johnny Q said, ''Lily, you'll be lookin' into your first
hunnerd-mile-an-hour fastball. I seen guys face square into
the cowhide when they're meanin' to back away. Somethin'
goes screwy. I ploughed a coupla guys' cheekbones in, Lily.
They just never moved.'' He looked at Eddie G as if to say
something else, I didn't know what. But Eddie G said:

''Are you ready, kid?''

At first I stood stock-still, just like the guys who took
Johnny Q's fastball in the face. I was afraid I hadn't really
heard the okay. But Eddie G had given me the okay for sure,
so I ran over to the platform, gripped the handrails, and
started up. I got to the tenth step, and Eddie G yelled:

''Stop!''

He yelled it in as loud a voice as I never knew he had. I
stopped. ''Look down at me now, Lily.''

I did. I smiled at him, and I gave a little wave. I heard
Johnny Q mumble, ''Shit,'' almost under his breath.

Eddie G said in a voice not so loud as before, but stern,
''Come down here right now!''

"Aw . . ."

"NOW!"

I did. I always did whatever he said. I stood before him again. His eyes were wider than a couple of portholes. "Lily, never let go again. You heard me warn you not to let go three or four times."

"I didn't let go."

"You waved."

"Hell, I was only up not even a regular flight of stairs."

"Watch that tongue."

"Sorry, Eddie G."

"Go back up and stop on the same step."

I ran back. I had learned a long time ago how to bear out my impatience with Eddie G's meticulous coaching. I didn't question him, and "question" included complaining and whining. But this was tough. I stopped at the tenth step and waited.

"Ten more, Lily."

I counted—one, two, three, four, five, six, seven, eight, nine, ten. I stopped. I could feel my heart thumping with anticipation. I could feel it thumping and hear it thumping, too. Ten more steps, Eddie G told me. At each stop, I'd look down and smile. I couldn't help smiling. I was so happy. And I said various things to them so Eddie G would know I wasn't scared.

"Nice weather up here. . . . Hey, I'm higher than the Alhambra. . . . Johnny Q! I can see the roof of the new Victor Hotel. . . . The Putty Man's truck's parked right out in front of it. . . ."

Eddie called out, "Pay attention to your feet and not the view, Lily. Look up toward the platform. You're almost there."

"Johnny Q!" I screamed. "The ocean. I can see all the way up to Palm Beach. The whole entire ocean, Johnny Q!" Johnny Q was looking back and forth between me and Eddie G. "The whole goddamned ocean!"

I had lost control of my mouth, I was so excited. I had reached the top of the platform, and I was jabbering like a maniac. I guess I'd stopped hearing Eddie G. For the first time ever, I wasn't paying attention to my coach. Now, I heard Johnny Q yell. He yelled, "No, no!" I looked down, and I saw the top of Eddie G's head turn ninety degrees, and he walked off toward the clubhouse door. I saw Johnny Q running after him. My coach was leaving me.

"Eddie G!" I screamed. "Eddie G, don't you leave me up here. Come back!" That's when I got scared. When my coach had gone and left me. Things began to sway. I was on the platform, and there was nothing to hold on to. I swear the platform started to tilt. "Eddie G! Help me!"

He came charging back. He shouted, "Here I am, Lily. I'm right here with you now, baby. You stand tall, and you take command of that platform. You take command!"

And Johnny Q, about to burst, yelled up all that he knew how to say. He screamed at me, "You're on the mound, Lily, you're on the mound. Just you. The game's all yours. It's a pitcher's game. . . . A PITCHER'S GAME! AND YOU'RE THE PITCHER!"

I looked out at the sea. A gull was circling not too far from shore. He stopped beating his wings in order to stay in one spot above some fish. Then he went into his dive. It was a great dive, but he sure made a splash. The fish got away. I yelled:

"Hey, Eddie G, there's a seagull out there forgot to adjust his left wing. Just made the sloppiest dive I ever did see."

"Well, you show him how, Lily! Show him how it's done."

I stepped to the edge of the platform, and my instructions, so ingrained, poured across the inside of my forehead. I found my spot, and I stared as hard at my spot in the pool as the seagull did at his fish. I raised my arms. The moment just before the one when you can't go back lasted a very long time. Eddie G willed me an extra fraction of a moment to make my decision. And as my body edged forward to the point of no return, some great flush of mightiness rose up from between my legs and spread through my whole body as I pushed off. The world shot up at me, and I imagined the seagull was watching and I showed him how it was done. The water smacked my head so hard I thought it was split open for sure, and I pushed my palms against the bottom of the pool so I could shoot back up before too much blood got into the water. I broke into the air, and a whoosh of breath came out of my mouth and I opened my eyes. There was no blood anywhere.

Damnedest thing happened. Eddie G and Johnny Q both jumped right into the pool with their shirts on. And then we were all hugging and kissing and congratulating and swallowing water, and I said, "Now let's get outa here so I can try a flip . . . or a back dive in a tuck position . . . or a—"

"Lily!"

That evening, the celebration with my mother was very special to me, because she wanted to know everything. She was so happy for me. She was believing in me more and more. She said she'd been afraid I wouldn't be able to do it, and I'd lose my confidence about all my spring-board diving, too. She said:

"Lily, tell me what it was like to soar through the air." She was like a little kid, and I suddenly felt older than my mother. But I didn't want to deprive her of her excitement, so I told her exactly what it was like. I said:

"The very first dive was the best of all, Ma. When I started sailing off that platform, my whole insides just exploded, starting right at my *weenie*!"

First there was silence, and then Johnny Q choked on his mouthful of whiskey. Eddie G turned red as a beet. And my mother started laughing and laughing till we all had to pound her on the back just as much as we had to pound on Johnny Q's. Then she hugged me and gave me a big loud smooch on the top of my head.

Johnny Q said this called for a real party.

It was a wonderful party, too. My mother, Johnny Q, Eddie G, and the Putty Man all went to Mr. Pancoast's park, and the Putty Man brought chicken in a basket. It turned out that Mr. Fraley was there with his family, having their own picnic. He had a large family—a large wife and seven kids. I knew two of the Fraley kids from school, and they offered me some of their mother's homemade root beer, so we all joined up and got one good softball game going. I got to pitch, and I was a good pitcher, though a very poor hitter. The older Fraley kids were excellent ballplayers, and Johnny Q gave them a lot of tips and they were grateful. This, along with the bottle of whiskey Johnny Q had polished off, made him cry. He said he never got a chance to teach his own kids the game of baseball.

Mrs. Fraley said to Johnny Q, "You've got the other eight folk on your team depending on you, Mr. Q, and the score is tied. So who's up?" My mother piped right up, "I am," which she wasn't. She wasn't even playing, just keeping score, but Johnny Q quick blew his nose, put her into the lineup, and the oldest Fraley boy got a little flustered pitching to a lady in a shimmy dress and high heels, so my mother drew a walk and we all cheered. I don't remember which team won the game.

As I grew taller and more slender, my muscles, of course, lengthened drastically. Eddie G could see this happening and had me adjust my new body to the board accordingly, and put in an extra hour a day, too. Adjusting takes up good practice time. So I became a more forceful diver than I'd been. This stage happened very fast. In six months. Adapting was my focus in the middle of my twelfth year. Not only did I have to readjust my changing body to the board, I had to adapt my mind to my body, too. In my child's mind, though, none of it was as tough as a few years back when I had to wear the wool bathing costume that weighed five pounds when it was wet.

I found it intriguing when Eddie G explained to me the elements that affected my flight and my entries. Any change of balance, no matter how infinitesimal, showed up, tenfold, in the entry. He explained that divers used little tricks to straighten out, but that I would not learn them.

"You have the sixth sense, Lily, remember that. The problems you're having now are worrisome, but you were born with what you need most, so I ain't gonna let you develop any crutches."

Johnny Q nodded.

Eddie G also said, "It's to do with timing. Stretch. Alignment. You're a natural, but now you have to work harder than ever. Can you work harder than ever, Lil?"

"I surely can, Eddie G."

A hundred dives a day, still, but now each one analyzed. Before school, after school, after dinner. Dive, dive, dive. I loved it.

When I was thirteen, Eddie G gave a long printed form to my mother. She had to give her permission for my first competition. Eddie G had waited for the right contest. He wanted an important one, and had let all the easy ones go by. He believed in beginner's luck. My mother called a conference. That was because the competition would take place at the Pancoast Club. The Pancoast Club was the most exclusive club on the beach. I was being sponsored by Mr. Fraley, who was a member. The Fraleys were becoming more and more our family friends. Our only family friends.

Mr. Fraley had come to Miami Beach about the same time as my mother and me. He'd been a steady customer of hers. He lived near the garage, at first, where we'd lived. His were the only kids I ever got to know very well in Miami Beach—my only playmates while I grew up. That was because of my spending so much time diving, of course, but also because there were not many kids around when all the building was going on. They never asked questions, the Fraley kids. They just played with me like I was their baby sister—built me sand castles, took me to the park. What was one more kid to them? Maybe Mr. Fraley warned them that they should be nice to me, but I don't think so. And that Mrs. Fraley made the best hot cross buns on Sunday mornings. What was one more hot cross bun to her? Mr. Fraley's investments paid off, and he got my mother and me into the Alhambra, which he'd financed. The Fraleys moved to the new Victor Hotel, in a whole suite of rooms.

So Mr. Fraley, since he was my sponsor, was in on my mother's conference. Johnny Q and Eddie G were glad to have him. They knew they needed someone legitimate to back up what they wanted to tell my mother. Suddenly, now that push had come to shove, she was resisting the idea of my competing. That was because she knew that if I beat those snobby rich kids, they'd be good and jealous and say God knows what to me. My mother decided the time had come for me to accept exactly what she was.

The three men didn't know that this was why she called the conference. Neither did I, naturally. None of us were prepared for what it was she had to say. At the conference, my mother started with:

"Lily, let's get this good and straight. Am I to understand that you want to compete against the kids on the North Beach in order to win the Miami Beach gold cup for diving?"

"Yes, Ma."

"Even if the other kids involved will be mean and nasty?"

"There are mean and nasty kids at school. I can take it."

"What do they do that's mean and nasty—the kids at school?"

"They don't really do anything. They say things that are mean and nasty."

"Like what?"

"They say I got no pop."

"What else?"

"I'm a bastard."

"And what do they mean by that?"

"Mrs. Cushman told me—she caught them—she said it was a derogatory word for a person who's got no pop. Like when Mrs. Cloak says she'll drop dead before some kike gets into the Alhambra. See, kike is a derogatory word for—"

Now, Eddie G and Johnny Q started giving each other glances. They turned their eyes to Mr. Fraley for guidance. He cleared his throat.

"Gert, you've always felt Lily didn't know what she was getting into. As far as competing. Now I'm beginning to get your drift here, but let me tell you this. Lily is a driven child. I know she is, because I'm what driven is. I came down here with eleven dollars and fifty cents in my pocket and a wife and a troop of kids. I worked eighteen hours a day to feed them, and two more to scrape enough money together to work on some deals. I've done a lot of bad things, and good things, too. But I made it. I'm a winner. Lily, you want to be a winner, too, don't you?''

"Yessir, Mr. Fraley."

He took my mother's hand. "She can do it, Gert. I can compare her to my own kids and see that. None of them's driven. Their old man was too busy to teach them drive. Lily is going to get you and herself out of this kind of hand-to-mouth living. You're still a spring chicken, Gert, but not for too much longer."

My mother said, "I have no intention of using my baby . . .''

Then she did something I'd never seen her do. Cry. Just burst into tears. When I think back, I believe she cried out of guilt. She knew I was her only way out. So I got up and snuggled into her lap, thought I was now a taller person than she. Her lap was as soft as it was when I was five.

"Ma, I know what Mr. Fraley's saying. Everyone's always talkin' about pulling themselves up by their boot-straps and stuff. But I'm only happy if you're happy, Ma. And all I know is I want to be a champion. I need you to want me to be a champion."

I did, too. I wasn't just trying to make her feel better. My mother told me later that I pronounced *champion* "champeen," just like Johnny Q.

She dried her eyes and looked deep into me. "Then let me tell you, champeen, what you're going to have to put up with in order to be one."

"Okay, Ma."

Then she said what I thought was the strangest thing.

"Lily, you know how babies are made, don't you?"

"Yes, Ma," though I didn't believe a word of it.

"When people do what you do to have babies, it feels awful good."

I didn't believe that, either, but I kept quiet. It wasn't the time to sass.

"It mostly feels good to the man," she said.

"How's that, Ma?"

Eddie G got up.

"Sit down, Eddie," my mother said. "Lily, that's something you can't understand yet. And it ain't easy to explain anyway. But sometimes it feels so good to certain men that they are willing to pay money to a woman to let them do it to them."

"So Mrs. Fraley must be pretty rich, right, Ma?"

My mother had to smack Johnny Q, he let out such a hoot.

"Now pay attention. Wives and husbands make babies without exchanging money. But when a man needs to . . . to make love to a woman . . . I mean, he sometimes has an uncontrollable urge. . . ."

"You mean Mrs. Fraley didn't like to do that stuff as much as Mr. Fraley?"

"Exactly."

I thought Mr. Fraley was going to be sick. I said, "But what's it got to do with love, Ma? A man sticks his weenie into a lady's weenie to make a baby. That's making a baby, not making love."

My mother sighed. Johnny Q was shaking his head, and Eddie G got up again. Mr. Fraley said, "Let me finish this, Gert."

"No, Richard. I will do it. Lily, get off my lap and make believe I'm your schoolteacher and you can't speak or raise your hand till I'm done."

"Okay, Ma." I slid onto my own chair.

"Honey, a woman who takes money from a man to let him make love to her—now that's just an expression that now you know the meaning of—that kind of woman is called a prostitute. Or a whore."

I'd seen the word *whore* plenty of times on notes kids passed me at school. *Yer ma's a hoor.* I looked up *hoor* in the dictionary, but couldn't find it.

"I can't let you go on not seeing the truth, Lil. Especially if I let these men set you up for what you'll have to face. I am a prostitute, Lily, because that's all I learned how to do. And I grew to like it, too. I like it, Lily, because I like the men who are my customers. They're my friends. And once we're . . . uh . . . done, then I don't have to answer to anyone.''

My mother was staring at me. She was waiting for me to say something. So I asked her, "How much do you get?"

Johnny Q slapped his thigh. My ma's eyes squinted as she looked into my eyes all the harder.

"Ask Mr. Fraley. Ask Johnny Q."

Johnny Q got all hurt. "Aw, Gert. We was friends. Lily, when I met your ma, we was friends, almost like a boy and his sweetheart. . . ."

"Lily, Johnny Q paid me by taking care of you."

I thought Johnny Q's eyes would pop out of his head. He jumped up. His mouth opened and shut like a washed-up fish. Then he sank back into his chair and put his big veiny face in his hands. Eddie G came over and put his hand on Johnny Q's shoulder. He said to me:

"This is too confusing for you, Lily. Your mother forgets that Johnny Q loves you like you're his own little gal. And he loves your mother, but she don't love him back. She uses him. Not the other way around." He looked at my mother. "If we're gonna get at the truth here, let's get at all of it."

Then there was a big shouting match. A huge adult argument with four adults. They forgot me. I watched them. I couldn't believe that Mr. Fraley or Johnny Q or even Eddie G, I guessed, ever put their weenies into my mother's. I knew someone must have, though. Thirteen years ago. My father. Whoever he was.

Mr. Fraley used his position of authority to calm things. He got them all to sit back down together, and my mother let him handle the rest of the conference.

"Lily, there are two things none of us wants to happen. For you to be hurt bad by the kids you'll be trying to beat out, and we especially don't want you to grow up to be . . . to be something you don't want to be."

"Ha! No chance there, Mr. Fraley. And I want my ma to know that I don't care about what anyone says to me. Sticks and stones will break my bones, but names will never hurt me. Besides, when they say I'm a bastard, I yell right back and tell them they're a bunch of dirty dog duties. And

I'll say this right now—I'm never gonna let a man stick his weenie in mine, ever. And, Ma, you told me that after this here conference, we'd go down to the Lincoln Theatre and see that Clark Gable movie we been waitin' on.'' My mother was mad about Clark Gable. ''Well, it's gettin' real late, and I'm gettin' embarrassed hangin' around here, and that's for sure!''

So that was the end of that—a lot of big sighs of relief. They apologized to me as if I were a grown-up lady, surprised that I would ever make such a speech. I usually just listened up. But I told them What For. I knew you couldn't apologize for what you were made of.

My mother and I went to see *It Happened One Night*. Before the lights went down, my mother went nuts over the Putty Man's mural. I'd been telling her about it, but she hadn't paid too much attention. The Putty Man had painted a big two-tone sun, and the line between the two colors was actually a floating naked lady. There were three more naked ladies under some strange-looking trees. I told my mother they were African trees. My mother said:

''What's the Putty Man know about Africa?''

''A lotta stuff. He said his great-granny told him exactly what Africa looked like. And he said he remembers every single word, 'cept his granny called Africa 'Molly.' Ain't that funny?''

She didn't say whether she thought Molly was a funny name for Africa, because the lights started to dim. During the *Eyes and Ears* and follow-the-bouncing-ball, we whispered in the dark about the conference. It was a lot easier talking in the dark about that stuff than talking in broad daylight in front of three men, all fighting.

''Ma, how come you don't have a lot of babies?''

''There are ways to make love and keep from getting pregnant.''

''Oh.'' I pictured Mr. Fraley with a little bitty cork in his weenie so no baby-making juice could leak out.

''Does Mrs. Fraley mind? I mean, about you?''

''Mr. Fraley thinks she doesn't know, and that's what she wants him to think.''

"I wonder why she doesn't like to make love as much as . . . as some other ladies do."

My mother sighed, then said, "Mr. Fraley isn't very good at it."

Good at it. Good at it must mean speedy.

"What about Eddie G?"

"What about him?"

"Does he pay you to do it with him?"

"He did once. But it didn't work out."

"Why not?"

"Well . . . he . . . he couldn't do it."

"No kidding?" Good for Eddie G.

"Shhh."

"I got a great coach, Ma."

"Hush now, Lily, and watch the picture."

I watched Clark Gable and Claudette Colbert. I tried to imagine Mr. Gable sticking his weenie into Miss Colbert's.

I still didn't believe it.

Chapter 5

For two years, I competed up and down Florida. I got better and better. I only lost when I tried too hard. Eddie G told me to do things just the way I did in my practices. That would be good enough to win. He was right.

The kids weren't mean to me after all. At least not in the way my mother was afraid they'd be. They ignored me. Their parents simply told their kids that I was lowlife. Oh, there were a couple of notes passed around the locker rooms. Rich kids know how to spell *whore*.

I grew even taller, and my hair began to darken a little so that the hair on my head was a golden blond and my braid almost white. Platinum, my mother said, like Jean Harlow.

I became very powerful. No one, Johnny Q told me, could come off the board with the force I generated. Because of my effort at springing off the board as high as I could get, my calves were almost as wide as my thighs. Not pretty, my mother said, but convinced herself that they only bulged out when I was up on my toes at the edge of the board. To feel powerful is a good feeling unlike any other. It's being invincible. It's being important. Maybe that's why the stuff that so worried my mother didn't get to me. I was too important.

My hips stayed narrow, but my backside seemed to round out more, hard as a medicine ball. In fact, Eddie G had incorporated the medicine ball, as well as weights, into my training. He could tell by my face that I hated it. Diving, even a hundred dives a day, was fun. Lifting and sweating was not. Weights took time away from the number of dives I did. I dropped to seventy-five a day.

I was actually quite fascinated with my body, as if it were something that was outside of me. I was watching it with interest as it changed. I believe when you focus so intensely on just one thing as I did with my sport, you become detached from anything else, because there isn't enough room in your brain to accommodate much else. I didn't menstruate till I was fourteen, and my nipples developed before I finally got breasts. My mother told me I was lucky to be so fashionably built. For two years, boys stared at the two flint arrow tips that stuck out of my chest. But then when I ended up with the two oranges, I got fewer stares.

Eddie G told me, once I'd developed, that his worries were over. He'd been afraid the change would be bad for my diving, like if my hips got real wide, or something like that. I never told him about the muscle pain I had, or the pulled feeling in my breasts, or the cramps. I just kept diving, adjusting—showing up that Casey the Cop doll.

My mother, once she realized how important each of the competitions was to me—the thought of missing one made me very upset—taught me how to put something in my weenie when I menstruated to soak up the blood. My mother had wanted to give me some medicine that would put off my cycle till after a competition, but Eddie G said, "No dice." He treated my menstruating no differently from eating, only you did it once a month instead of three times a day.

In 1935, the Olympic trials were held in Los Angeles. I was going, but first I was going to New York for some intensive training. I couldn't believe such a thing as leaving Miami Beach. I really couldn't remember New Haven, except for the pattern of blue and white stars on a ball that I and the cats played with at Granny's, and the time I saw a baby bird get run over by the back wheel of the milk truck. And I thought I remembered one cat—a blue cat—that could talk. That one really made my mother laugh, but laugh in a curious way. So I asked her what was so funny, but she just became her tight-lipped self the way she always did when I asked her about my granny.

My mother was very excited about going on our trip. The Miami Beach Bath Club would pay our expenses. Her excitement was the only thing that was real about the trip. But then, suddenly, everything collapsed like a blown-up paper bag getting smashed with a fist. I learned that Eddie G wouldn't be coming.

One morning at the pool, a man in a Panama suit and straw boater and spats whom I'd seen around all week was sitting at a table with Eddie G. Johnny Q was a few yards away, waiting. Eddie G told me to sit down and introduced me to the man.

"Lily," he said, "this is Mr. Marvin Modeen. He will be taking you to New York."

"Nice to meet you." I figured now that we were heading for the big time, Eddie G had gone and hired some kind of manager for us.

"He is your new coach."

Mr. Modeen and I were still in the middle of a handshake when Eddie G said these ridiculous words. I don't know what I said. Something awful. But I ran away right after whatever it was I said. Johnny Q caught up with me out on the sand in front of the Flamingo. I'd run quite a long way. He put his arm around me, and his callused palm scratched my shoulder. He said:

"This is the big one, Lil."

I didn't look up at him. I just kept staring at the horizon.

"And we're all small-time here."

Now, I looked up at him. "No, we're not. You're not small-time, Johnny Q. Nobody's thrown a fastball like yours in twenty years."

"You're forgettin' the Diz."

"He stinks."

" 'Course he don't stink. Hey, Lil, my pitchin' days was too long ago for me to remember how it felt to be the best. Now, it's you who's the best. You're goin' up to New York with Mr. Modeen. And your ma will be with you the whole way.''

"Well, I don't see why she doesn't stay here, so I can have Eddie G come.''

"That's what your ma said, too.''

"She did?''

"She thought Eddie G could be Mr. Modeen's assistant. She wasn't thinkin' right, though. And she ain't here this mornin' with us, because she said she couldn't stand to see you hear this. She sure does love you, Lily. You can always tell when someone really loves ya. They're never there when you need them the most.''

Johnny Q waited for me to say something, but I didn't. I was trying to understand.

"If somebody who really loves ya is there when you want them more than anything, they're a crutch. A crutch that holds you back. And you know what Eddie G's told you about crutches. And, Lil, I had to tell your ma that if the two of you are ever separated, you'd never get back together. Someone up in New York would take you away once they seen the talent you got, the money they could make off ya. I know all about that. And besides, Eddie G can't take you no further than where you are now, even if he wanted to.''

"I can't be taken no further by anyone.''

"Nobody's better than Modeen. Eddie's worked hard to get him to come see ya, Lily. Modeen has just sent his best star diver packin'. He knows you're somethin' real special.''

"And who's gonna pay for Modeen? He can't come cheap, not with that suit he's got on.''

"The winners, Lily, get taken care of. While Mr. Modeen takes care of you, he'll be taken care of by the Olympic backers in Los Angeles soon as you place in the trials. And Modeen wouldn't take you on if he wasn't cocksure. Lily, you've come all this way. Don't be a loser.''

I looked up at him. "I ain't a loser. But neither are you, Johnny Q.''

He bent over and picked up a little dried-up starfish. He

gave it to me. "No, I ain't, Lily. Because of you, though, not because of me."

Then he seemed to shake a little, and he squatted down on his haunches the way he did when he drank. I squatted down, too. I pressed the starfish against my mouth to keep it shut. I didn't want to say something stupid, as I knew I would.

Johnny Q wiped his eyes, then he said, "Don't you take your divin' away from me, Lily. Don't you do it. And most of all, don't take it away from Eddie G. Especially not away from Eddie G."

"Hey. What's the matter, Johnny Q?"

He stood up. He picked up a chunk of coral. He drew back and threw it out over the ocean. It skimmed along, three inches above the water, and when you could barely make it out, it curved up and just kept on going. I couldn't imagine what kind of pitch Johnny Q must have had in his prime. Better than Dizzy Dean for sure. Johnny Q said:

"There's just a lot you don't know; a lot you don't know about your ma. These fellas she's been with lately—they're a bad crew. Seems their way of gettin' to Easy Street is fixin' boxing matches. Lil, you ain't suffered adult sufferin'. Kids don't know about sufferin' even when they're sufferin'. A kid is like a worm in the horseradish—thinks it's a great place, 'cuz he ain't been nowheres else. You just go on up to New York with Mr. Modeen and then on to Los Angeles, and me and Eddie G will be watchin' the *Eyes and Ears of the World*, lookin for ya."

I said, though weakly, and it was a lie, "I don't want to go."

" 'Course you do. You're gonna be the champeen!"

He smiled.

"And I sure don't like that Mr. Modeen and his white spats."

"And you shouldn't. Player shouldn't like his coach and vice versa. Player should just respect his coach's knowledge. And when you train these next coupla weeks with Modeen, you'll respect the hell out of each other for sure."

"But I like Eddie G. I *love* Eddie G!"

"That's different."

"How come?"

He stood. "Let's go back now, Lily. Mr. Modeen wants to talk to you."

As we walked back down the beach, I asked Johnny Q, "Will Eddie G at least help Mr. Modeen while he's down here in Florida?"

"Yeah. He'll help him by stayin' outa the way. Athlete can't have but one coach."

I didn't say anything, because there was nothing left to say. But then I thought of something.

"Do you think Ma'll stop being a prostitute once she's outa the horseradish?"

He hooted. "She'll stop, Lily. She'll hafta. But she'll be throwin' her charms around at those Olympic people. You two are gonna have a lotta fun."

"What about Mr. Modeen?"

"What about him?"

"Will he pay my ma to do stuff with him?"

"I believe that'll be up to you, Lil."

"Me?"

"Yeah. Tell your ma she can't, that's all. Comin' from you, she'll know how important it is that she stay away, like Eddie G already knows."

I looked at the green-blue ocean. Me tell my ma? That was something new. Two new things thrown at me in just one morning. I said:

"Shee-it!" and I kicked a piece of coconut shell.

"Now you stop that cursin', Lily. You're goin' to California to make the Olympic team. And they don't want no kid representin' the good ole U.S. who swears like a truck driver."

"Okay, Johnny Q, okay. I'll do it. And I'm gonna do it right. But let's take a quick dip, first. Whadya say? A race?"

"Yer on!"

I took off my sandals, put my starfish into the right one, and lay them side by side in the sand. Johnny Q took off his old drunk guy's shoes. I wasn't supposed to swim in my clothes, especially, I was sure, in the new sundress my

mother had bought for me to wear when I met Mr. Modeen.
I hoped it'd be ruined good.

Mr. Modeen had been pretending to be a guest at the club
for five days before I met him. He'd been studying Eddie G
putting me through my paces. Now, for a few more days,
he continued to watch, writing in a big black notebook the
whole time. He soon filled the entire notebook up with his
scribble. Then it took me a week to go through the notebook
with him.

Eddie G watched him as he took me through the notebook. The first time that I informed Mr. Modeen that what
he was making me do was different from the way Eddie G
had me do it, he gritted his teeth. I felt good that he had to
grit his teeth to stay calm. The thing he was telling me to
do wasn't really too different from the way Eddie G had me
do it, but I wanted to see how he'd react. I figured he'd get
mad, because my mother told me the one thing men hated
was to be compared to other men. She warned me not to
do what I'd just done.

He put his notebook aside. He said, "From the beginning, I have called you Miss Neelan over your protests. You
know my first name, but you have the sense that I don't
wish you to use it. We are purely a business partnership,
Miss Neelan. A professional partnership. And I believe that
you are smart enough to know this, even though you are
quite immature in many ways. So don't test me again, and
I won't test you. I expect you to act grown up. Your childhood is officially over. Now, then, Edward Greene has raised
you to be a good diver. An excellent—"

"Who?"

He ignored me. ". . . diver. He was fortunate to have
gotten you at such a young age, and you were certainly
fortunate as well. Mr. Greene has done a superb job considering what he had to face up to back when he was a
young man. But his job is over. It is now my job to shape
you to conform to what the judges will be looking for. Your
first coach, Edward Greene, built you. I will polish you. I
have been looking for a diver like you for years. And I've

looked all over this country, too. I have chosen you because you have the most potential of any I've seen. Now, I must ask you to choose, too. Do you choose me, Miss Neelan?''

I never hesitated. Not for a second. I had just had my first formal lesson in respect. I said, ''I do choose you, Mr. Modeen.''

''Good. We will call it a day. Tomorrow the photographer comes. Ever been in a movie, Miss Neelan?''

''No, sir, Mr. Modeen.''

''You will be tomorrow. And I can assure you that you will soon be fearfully bored with watching yourself dive, but we must take advantage of the high state of the motion-picture industry that is available to us. It will give us an edge. Athletic coaches are conservative people. I am not. I want to have the best diver in the world next year. And I intend to get it.''

I didn't like being an It too much, but this was a business relationship after all.

I swear I sweat even in the pool under the water. Mr. Modeen had to give me special eyewash, because the whites of my eyes turned red. And when I wasn't diving, instead of weights, Mr. Modeen had me out in the ocean swimming against the undertow. While I was nearly getting drowned, Mr. Modeen would stand there at the edge of the ocean in his damned Panama suit and holding his extra-damned boater hat, and I'd be out there wishing and hoping a wave could surprise him and soak his white spats. That didn't happen. Without looking down, he was able to step back and avoid the lip of foam at the last second every time.

Before, when Eddie G would sometimes get frustrated with my not understanding what adjustment he'd want me to make, he'd do some demonstration dives. He'd say from the board, ''Now Lily, watch the position of my elbows just before I go into my reverse.'' I couldn't remotely imagine Mr. Modeen in a pair of bathing trunks. But then, he had his movies. And his movies were a tremendous help to me. What I couldn't feel, I could see. Even though they were more instructive than Eddie G's demonstration dives, I, of course, didn't tell Mr. Modeen that.

The first time I saw a movie of myself diving, I said, "Whoo-ee. I am good, Mr. Modeen, ain't I?"

Mr. Modeen said, "Not as good as you will be."

My new coach let me continue my pitching practice with Johnny Q. He was curious about that. He wasn't quite sure exactly what that did for my diving, but he knew it didn't hurt. I told him it kept my arms from looking like sissy arms. When I said that, he squinted his eyes and thought—stood there thinking for five or ten minutes. Then he walked away and wrote in his black notebook. I asked him what he was writing, and he said, "My theories on what all that throwing has done for you . . . in terms of . . ." He looked up at me. "Never you mind, Lily. Yours is not to know why." Dismissed. I didn't like the idea of being turned into a Casey the Cop doll. It's one thing to learn something from a windup toy, but not so nice to be turned into one.

I told my mother how I felt about that. She just laughed, and said, "When you win an Olympic medal, Lil, then it'll be your turn to wind up Mr. Modeen and send him on his way."

Mr. Modeen took my mother and me to dinner one night to give us ". . . the details of train travel, the hotel situation, and training schedules." It was the first time he'd ever really talked with my mother at any length, and we were five minutes into cocktails when I could see he was smitten. My mother was wearing pink and black. The restaurant in the Flamingo Hotel was silver. She looked like a million. She gazed across the candlelight, her Pink Lady raised just below chin level, her pink nails frosted silver, and she blew a thin stream of smoke out between her wet lips. She said, "I surely hope, Marvin, that once in New York, I won't be in the way." She tilted her head.

I said, "Excuse me."

"Yes, Lily," my mother said, not taking her eyes off Mr. Modeen.

"Coach's name, Ma, is *Mister* Modeen."

Her beautiful face turned toward me. I watched her reading my eyes. I think at that moment it was her turn to choose. Marvin or Mr. Modeen. Was she going to keep being a prostitute, or drop it long enough to just be a mother? Mr. Modeen, a shrewd man even when smitten, read the tension. So he said:

"A certain formality is, of course, required at the New York Athletic Club. I'm sure, Mrs. Neelan, that abandoning the informality of your lovely beach town will come as easily to you as it has to your daughter . . . once you're there."

My mother got his meaning, and I got it, too. He'd have a nice little tryst here in Florida with my mother—that was okay with him—but then it was strictly business. My mother's eyes were wide, wider-looking than most humans', because she curled and stiffened her lashes. She gave Mr. Modeen one of her dazzling smiles. "Why, sir, you must forgive me. However, may I assure you that the two ladies you will be accompanying to New York will meet all your requirements of formality. And Lily is correct. We will start adapting to the big city's cultural habits immediately . . . Mr. Modeen."

That night, when my mother tucked a sheet over me and kissed my cheek, she said, "Be patient with me, Lily. I'm one of those old dogs you can't teach new tricks to."

"Ma?"

"Yes, Lily?"

"Did you mean to say tonight that once we set out for New York, you will stop doin' it?"

"Doin' it?" She was playing for time.

"Yeah." She got her extra second, which was all my mother ever needed to formulate her decisions.

"Listen, Lil, you are almost a woman, you know. Almost. And once you are, I will no longer interfere in your life. I am a woman who's already made her choices. You may not interfere in my life."

"But . . ."

"Lily, rest assured I will not obstruct your course. And you will not be embarrassed by me. I am not going to be a prostitute once we leave this town, but I'm gonna have fun. Okay?"

I thought about that.

"And if it will make you feel better, I am ready to settle in with one man. One who can afford us. Once we leave, I will start looking."

"You're going to get married, Ma?"

She laughed. "Marriage, Lily, made my mother a crazy woman."

"But it wouldn't make you a crazy woman, Ma."

"I'm afraid it would. Did I ever tell you about the time I almost got married?"

She surely hadn't. "Ma, really?"

"Really. I was a very young girl. Almost as young as you. A hard-working, ambitious young fellow showed an interest in me. I may have been from the wrong side of the tracks, but I was a very attractive girl. And his family hadn't been on the right side of the tracks for very long. So he courted me, and one day I sat with him and with his mother on their front porch. We were sitting on the glider, and we rocked back and forth, and enjoyed the sweetest breeze from a rose hedge nearby. Yes, I decided then, this was the life for me. Sittin' and glidin' and smellin' the roses. Then he asked his ma for an apple. I said, 'Oh, Harry, let me get it for you.' I was kind of in the mood for an apple myself."

She stopped, and began to examine a chipped nail.

"What happened?"

"Well, I went and got two apples, and I came out on the porch and held out his apple to him, and he just stared at me as if I was offering him a handful of mothballs. And I said, 'What is it, Harry?' And Harry said, in this most peculiar tone of voice, 'Why, it isn't peeled.' "

My mother didn't say anything else, so I said, "Oh."

I waited and she still didn't say anything else, so I said, "I guess you shoved it right down his throat, and then he didn't want to marry you, right, Ma?"

She smiled a Cheshire grin. "Not quite that, Lily. I've always been a bit more subtle in my approach to men than you. I told him that apples didn't come off the trees peeled. Then his mother right away jumped up to peel it for him, all nervous about a fight starting, so I just walked off the porch eating my apple. Then I realized why my mother had gone nuts. Women aren't really meant for marriage, Lily.''

"Well, Ma," I said, "I'm sure there's lot of men who wouldn't be so demanding.''

"They are all demanding, and humiliation so often goes along with the demands that it's a wonder women aren't all crazy. Anyway, I decided that if men were going to place unreasonable demands upon me, they'd have to pay me for them. I've peeled a lot of apples for men like Harry since, Lil, but such service ain't free.

"And now, Lily, the more I think about all this New York stuff, the more I have come to realize that it's time for us to move on. These fellows I've met lately, these guys with the funny names . . .''

"Louie the Lip?''

"Yeah. Well, those guys are a little rough. I think they're expecting just a little bit more of me than I'm willing to give. And I have to be the boss.''

I became downcast. I wasn't sure what she was talking about, but I knew it wasn't good. So my mother lifted my chin with her hand. "But if and when I find that sugar daddy I'm lookin' for, he and I will be peelin' apples for each other, and for you, too.''

She went to the door and turned off my light. "Ma?''

"Yes, darlin'?''

"Not Mr. Modeen though, right, Ma?''

"No need to worry, Lily. I flirted with Mr. Modeen tonight because the gin made me all cozy. But that Mr. Modeen, though an up-and-comin' fella for sure, is not the kind of man I'm lookin' for. I want somebody who's already up.''

"And, Ma, who knows,'' I said, "maybe you'll even marry such a fella, seein' as he's up.''

"Gotta find him first, Lil. Then we'll go on from there. Nighty-night, baby.''

She shut my door.

Chapter 6

I didn't say good-bye to Johnny Q or Eddie G or anybody else. My mother said she'd talked it over with them, and they all agreed that they'd treat the day of my leaving for New York just like any other, except instead of going to the pool I'd be going to the train. They said that the next time I'd see them, we'd all say hello like no time had gone by at all. And there was my mother going along, knowing that if things worked out the way she was hoping, we would never see either of them again.

It's a good thing I didn't know what she was planning. I would never have won anything if I'd known my mother would do such a thing as try to take my home and my family away, strange home and strange family though they might have been.

Maybe I should have figured out what was going on in her mind by the way my mother was packing. She picked up or touched every single thing in our apartment. Some stuff she'd wrap and put into one of our trunks, and some stuff she'd sigh over and pass by. She said, "Want to take the Putty Man's little statues, Lily?"

"No, Ma, just leave them on the shelf. I don't want them getting smashed."

My mother, without my knowing it, during the night before we left, wrapped each little sculpture, and stored them all with her makeup. We had to leave very early next morning while it was still dark, so I didn't notice them gone from one end of my shelf. Even though she figured she was doing what she thought was best for us, knowing it was cruel, she was doing it from love and duty. I always knew that, even when I was so angry with her when I realized how she'd tricked me.

Besides the two trunks, my mother had four suitcases, mostly full of her hunting equipment. She had big game to stalk this time. She spent a lot of money on clothes before we left, and planned to spend a lot more once in New York.

We traveled in a first-class compartment on the Silver Meteor. A Pullman is a nice place to sleep. The curtains drifting back and forth with the train's motion made me feel snug. Mr. Modeen continued coaching me on the train, telling me all the things I had to remember and making me repeat his reminders back. My mother, now calling herself a gay divorcée rather than a widow, fell in with a crowd of swells who spent the whole time in the lounge car. They didn't sleep in their Pullmans at night. Neither did my mother. They waited for the sun to come up first.

In the time of the Great Depression, there were a lot of people who made do without knowing where their next meal was coming from, and then there were the kind of people my mother got to know on the train. People who ran about here and there, and whose money must have been stored somewhere in big buckets, because they peeled bills off their rolls as if it weren't worth more than water. My mother didn't find the right sugar daddy on the train, but she had a wonderfully good time. Her train friends told her she was a real glamour girl.

Only once in all the time I was with Mr. Modeen was he kindly to me, and that was on the train. By "kindly" I mean that he stopped being so stiff and cold, which was the kind of person he decided he had to be in order to be up-and-coming. One morning after breakfast when he was reading to me from his notebook, I started crying for no reason. He stopped reading and gave me his handkerchief. He said, "Everyone feels blue once in a while. You cry for a while, and I'll be back." For Mr. Modeen, this was kindly. But when he came back, I was still crying. He said, "Why don't you try to figure out what is making you cry, Miss Neelan, and then say what it is, and then it will be done.''

So I said how bad it would be if I didn't make the team. How terrible my mother would feel, and how terrible Johnny Q and Eddie G would feel. Then my mother came in and asked, ''What's up?''

Mr. Modeen said, ''She's feeling punk about the possibility of letting everyone down.'' Mr. Modeen could deal with everything so far except my feeling sad. He left me with my mother.

My mother told me that I could never let her down. Because of me, she was getting a free trip to Gotham, she said. And she told me I'd given Johnny Q and Eddie G a new lease on life. I said, ''What's a new lease, Ma?''

''Lily, you don't remember old Johnny Q when you first met him. He was one wreck of a man. You've reminded him of good times gone by—he never thought he'd know good times again.''

Then my mother started talking about Eddie G. The words, when I try to think back on them, become all blurred together, just like the backyards of North Carolina as they flew by the window. She told me that Eddie G had come back from the dead—had been a human zombie till he got interested in coaching me.

She said that he had come to her one day—a few weeks after he'd met up with his old pal Johnny Q. Johnny Q had been working on him to teach me to be a diver. Eddie G didn't know what to do. So my mother settled in with him and he told her he'd once had a small son and that he'd wanted his son to be the greatest diver the world had ever seen. But then he went and introduced him to the platform before the boy was ready. The boy wasn't prepared well enough—wasn't old enough. Eddie G told my mother how he'd hurried the boy because he was more concerned with his own personal prestige. And little Eddie, wanting more than anything to please his pop, went and jumped off the platform though he was scared out of his wits, and he broke his neck.

Eddie G paid my mother his money so he'd have someone to talk to—so he could tell someone that he'd killed his son.

My mother and I both sat there in the train hugging and crying. She told me she held Eddie G in her arms the very same way we were doing and rocked him and told him it was an accident. And she told him that she trusted him to teach me to be a diver. She wouldn't take any money from him once she'd gotten him calmed down, either.

So when Mr. Modeen came back, my mother and I were both pretty hysterical, clutching onto each other for dear life, her saying over and over how Eddie G didn't want me to know about little Eddie.

She said, ''Lily, though I kept tellin' that poor Eddie G how it was an accident, Eddie G said he could never stop blamin' himself for letting such a thing happen. And, Lil, he's still blamin' himself, but because of you, at least he's not doing it every damnable second of the day.''

Mr. Modeen went out again but came right back—this time with a big glass of Moxie for me and a highball for my mother. Then he stopped being kindly. He reminded us of how little time there was left, and how we had a great deal of work to do. So my mother dabbed at her eyes with her perfumed lace hankie and got me a cold washcloth.

I had always known I had a lot of work to do. For my mother and for Johnny Q and for Eddie G. But now I was thinking of little Eddie, too. And so my determination grew all the more.

Mr. Modeen and I went directly from Penn Station to the New York Athletic Club, and my mother to our rooms at the Taft. The only part of New York I saw was in the taxi between the club and the Taft every morning before rush hour and every evening after rush hour. Mr. Modeen had me training four hours in the morning, four in the afternoon, and two at night. I wished I could go to the Empire State Building or to the planetarium or maybe up to a New York Giants game at the Polo Grounds, where Johnny Q had been a pitcher to be reckoned with, but Mr. Modeen told me I wasn't in New York to see the sights. After I'd

made the team, he said, then he'd lighten up my schedule.
So I put the New York Giants out of my mind.

But one day my mother came after my morning workout
to the little room where Mr. Modeen and I had our meals
and where I had my rest breaks. My mother had on her
widest-brimmed straw hat with a red scarf attached, and she
sailed it across the room from the doorway and it made a
perfect three-point landing on my cot. My mother was
working on her entrances herself. Mr. Modeen looked up
from his chair at his desk.

"Mr. Modeen," she said, "my girl will not be training
with you this afternoon. But I promise she'll be to bed early
and be bright and chipper come morning practice." She
pulled me toward the door by my hand.

Mr. Modeen stood up and pulled my other hand. "Now
wait a minute, Mrs. Neelan. Lily will be competing in less
than two weeks."

"Good. Then you've plenty of time left."

"On the contrary, Mrs. Neelan . . ."

"She needs a half-day break. And so do you, Mr. Modeen. You look like an old rummy."

That was true. He was standing there all disheveled, and
was sweaty and ragged. Of course, my mother was speaking
in her hunting voice, a voice accompanied by little gestures
and a small pout that made men turn to mush. I piped up:

"I do think I'd like to get everything out of my head, Mr.
Modeen, and tomorrow everything will come rushing back
all fresh. Things are startin' to blur."

"She needs some sun, Mr. Modeen."

"Well, just what are you planning, then? I can't have her
overstimulated. She's on a nice steady keel. . . ."

"Where she will stay, most positively. Come, Lily, you
mother wants you to see something very special."

"See what, Ma?" Silently, I begged she'd say, "The view
from the Empire State Building."

"The *Normandie*, Lily. The *Normandie* is about to arrive!"

"Oh." I'd seen a million ships at the Miami cut.

"The *Normandie* is the biggest, most beautiful ship in all

the world, and it's coming in from its maiden voyage to-day.''

"Will we get to go on it, Ma?" I asked, trying to sound excited.

"Not today, I hope, Mrs. Neelan," Mr. Modeen called from the doorway. "There will be all sorts of people crushing . . .''

"No, Mr. Modeen, not today. Lily's got to win her medals before they'll let us on the *Normandie*."

She grabbed her hat and could see that I was looking disappointed. She said, "Even Mickey Mouse will be in the harbor today, Lily!" She hugged me.

Once I was out in the streets of New York, the *Normandie* was all I heard people talking about. She was coming in, flying the blue riband. The riband was a long, thin strip of blue silk, and to fly it meant she was the fastest liner in the world. She was breaking the Italian Line's record. What my mother was doing was this—she was setting out to see me inspired.

A New York City cop got my mother and me the best seat in the house—atop the roof of an eight-story warehouse directly across the street from the West Forty-eighth Street pier where the *Normandie* was to dock. Because the roof was filled with New York City cops' friends, we were mostly in the company of some very important gangsters. My mother recognized several of Lucky Luciano's buddies whom she'd known in Miami Beach. They even gave up a couple of chairs they'd dragged up there. I felt as if my mother were the queen of New York, and I was the royal princess.

One fellow had a radio, and we listened to the excited newscaster describing the *Normandie* as it entered the harbor and passed the Statue of Liberty. The newscaster shouted:

"And what a SIGHT as one GREAT lady from FRANCE passes another. I BELIEVE the LADY of the HARBOR holds her LIGHT just a bit HIGHER today. Ah . . . the

FRENCH . . . THE FRENCH!'' You could tell he really was thrilled to death.

Then we could see it coming up the Hudson, and it was as if we were watching a rocket ship land on the moon. It was as majestic as a cathedral. On the streets below, people cheered wildly and bands played. The great ship was accompanied up the river by Coast Guard cutters, excursion steamers, and a huge sidewheeler that surely didn't look very huge next to the *Normandie*. There was a four-masted schooner, fireboats spraying towering arcs of water, all sorts of cabin cruisers and little fishing boats. A blimp floated across the sky, under the airplanes that had photographers hanging out of them taking pictures for the newspapers. The tugs began sending out blasts of steam, and there in the middle of it all was a long barge supporting a five-story-high balloon in the form of Mickey Mouse. People said that the year before Macy's had held a parade on Thanksgiving Day, and the marchers were people holding mammoth balloons of cartoon characters. Mickey was from the parade. My mother and I were jumping up and down, and we didn't even know we were until we saw that even the gangsters were jumping up and down. They looked so funny. My mother said, ''God, I don't remember the last time I felt such a thrill.''

I felt a thrill every time I dived without a single error of form.

The ship went past us up the river and began to make her mind-boggling turn in order to maneuver cleanly into her berth. As she approached again, her back end bumped the pier, and five little tugboats lined up along her front end like little puppies sucking on their mother. They nudged her into place, and I actually thought for a second that she wouldn't be able to stop and she'd plow right through the building we stood on and us, too. Her bow seemed as skinny as a pencil.

A sixth little tug seemed to be in command of the others, and I said to my mother, ''Look at that tug, Ma. It has a gold eagle sitting on the pilot house.''

A gangster said, ''Twenty-eight-karat gilt. That's an old

tug. City can't afford that kind of thing on the new ones."
He smiled wistfully. "My pop used to work down here
'round these dirty piers."

I sort of mumbled to myself, "At least you had a pop."
My mother didn't hear me, either, though I wished she had
and was glad she hadn't at the same time.

Then everyone on the roof went and took the tour of the
ship for fifty cents. I asked, "Can we take a tour, Ma?"

"No, Lily."

"Mr. Modeen would like to kill us if we did, right?"

"Ha! Mr. Modeen couldn't kill a bug. He's a good coach,
but he's a fake. Sometimes I wonder where he gets his blus-
ter. But never mind that." She crossed her arms and got a
fierce expression on her face. "Lil, dollface, we are going
to tour that ship all right, but as passengers. Next year,
when we come home from Europe, we're gonna be first-
class passengers aboard that ship, you mark my words."

"Aw, Ma, how we gonna afford that?"

"I've told you, Lily, when you win your gold medals,
we'll be able to afford whatever we want."

"We're gonna melt the medals down, Ma?"

She laughed. "No, honey. Ya see, if you win, the crème
de la crème are gonna want us to ride their magic carpets
with them. High society will be payin' our way."

"Ma?"

"Yes, Lily?"

"What if I don't win?"

She put her arm around my waist as if we were two
chums. "You're my gal, Lil, win or lose. But if you lose,
it's gonna be one helluva swim, now ain't it?"

She gave me a squeeze.

I looked at the little tug with the gold eagle. I promised
it I'd win a gold medal for my mother. Maybe two, if Mr.
Modeen could figure out a way to simmer down my exhil-
aration coming off the platform. He told me my mental ex-
hilaration showed up in my line. I was working hard on that.

When we were through staring at the big ship, my mother
took me to the Automat to get something to eat. I chose a
piece of lemon-meringue pie. It must have been eight inches

high. In New York, not just the buildings are bigger than
everywhere else. Before we got a taxi to go to the Taft, we
walked back to the pier to see the *Normandie* one more
time. Dusk had come, and the commotion had subsided.
The sun turned the Hudson orange as it set behind the liner.
We watched the *Normandie*'s lights go on until every porthole was a brilliant yellow circle. It was so beautiful. We
started to walk to the taxi stand when I looked over my
shoulder in time to see the hundreds of light bulbs go on
across the ship's riggings and the ones atop the ship spelling
out her name, THE NORMANDIE.

"Oh, Ma! Look!"

She turned, and her mouth fell open. "Now ain't that
somethin'!"

"Reminds me of Miami Beach, Ma. As bright as the top
of the Flamingo." The Flamingo Hotel has a dome made
of ground glass, and when the sun hits it, it's as though you
are looking into heaven.

She pulled me away as if she didn't want to be reminded
of Miami Beach. I figured she was probably as homesick as
I was.

Chapter 7

The night before we arrived back in New York from Europe, Captain Pugnet threw a soiree for about fifty of us. F. Scott Fitzgerald was there, and his wife winked at me again. Alice Roosevelt and my mother got on swell. It was the first time I ever saw my mother talk more than three words to another woman. I asked my mother what they were laughing at and talking about for so long. She said, "Men."

I finally got to see the movie stars, and they were very glad to see me. They looked like ordinary people. I shook hands with Laurence Olivier and Mr. and Mrs. Fairbanks and Leslie Howard and Kitty Carlisle. Cary Grant was very kindly toward me and told me he wished he had my concentration. I felt as if I were dreaming. One year before, when I took the train out of Miami with Mr. Modeen, I left Mr. Grant's picture on my wall. And now I was talking to him. He was very nice.

Mr. Henderson of *The New York Times* was finally allowed by my mother to interview me. He asked me what I'd enjoyed most about the Olympics. I said:

"The most exciting thing was when that Archie Williams spread the rumor that I was an albino Negro. Whoa, did that start all sorts of—"

"Lily," my mother interrupted, "perhaps the most exciting thing was when you marched into the stadium on opening day in your very snazzy uniform and felt like part of—"

Now, Mr. Henderson interrupted my mother. "Miss Neelan, you have won two gold medals in the Olympic Games. Is there anything else in the world a girl could possibly wish for?"

"Yes. I wish Jesse Owens and my friend Archie Williams were here on the *Normandie*. We could've held some races for the crew up on the first promenade, and had a real good time. All the passengers could have come up to watch, brought up their deck chairs. . . ."

My mother right away took Mr. Henderson aside. I watched her charm him. She talked to him and leaned her left breast into his arm while she spoke in a voice too quiet for anyone but the two of them to hear. When she came back, her face was very hard. She was mad at me. That's because you can't charm a *New York Times* reporter. Which is why they work for *The New York Times* and not the *Mirror*. Mr. Henderson refused to retract what would be the lead line in his story.

My mother said, "Lily, please don't mess things up now. We're so close."

I was tired of not understanding. That was when I decided that though it wasn't necessary to understand why my coach was telling me to do things, I should know what all my mother was talking about. I said, "Mess up what, Ma? Too close to what?"

"Oh, Lily! Why didn't you just tell Mr. Henderson that the only thing you wished for now was your Prince Charming."

"But I ain't wishin' for Prince Charming."

My mother put the back of her hand to her forehead. She didn't understand me because I had always been so complacent. And she didn't know that my complacency was because I never knew what people were meaning. My mind was too deep into diving to try to sort out what people expected of me outside of my diving, or what I was supposed to say. My mother was all the madder: "Don't use that tone, Missy."

She had never called me that before. That was how Mrs. Cloak talked to the colored cleaning people. But right away, my mother heard what her own tone sounded like and she sort of sagged. She put her arm around my waist. "Listen, Lil, I felt bad for all those colored boys too. I did. I still do. Please believe me. But their problems are theirs and we have ours."

"We do?"

She stared at me. She took my arm, and we left the captain's private party room and went to the deck rail outside. It was windy as a hurricane. My mother's chiffon shoulder drapes blew out over the rail. She said:

"I have protected you with all I could muster, Lily. So have Johnny Q and Eddie G. When I got too involved with those boxing characters and things were lookin' real bad, I didn't care what they did to me, but I was so terrified of them finding out that I had you. We must have protected you too much, Lily. Now, I am beginning to see that you don't know anything besides leaping off a plank of wood." She was pretty tipsy. She told me the next day—as a way of apologizing—that she shouldn't drink so much. "Lily, when I was your age walking up and down Spring Street—that's a road that goes through the warehouses down by the docks in Bridgeport—I was turning tricks. At fifteen. Now I'm sayin' that thinkin' you know what it means."

"I do."

"You don't. I've done too good a job protecting you. *Too* good a job. Lily, you're going to be sixteen in a week. You've got to know how terrible it was to do the things I did with men . . . for . . . for two bits! That's all I could get when I was pregnant. Men with blood and fish guts on their—"

"Ma!"

She reached for me and hugged me tight. "Oh, Lily, you and me only have each other. Together, we can make sure that that kind of living stays behind us. Far behind. Now you display your medals proudly and you smile for the photographers and you stop talking about Jesse and Archie and Mr. Hitler and the Jews and all that stuff nobody wants to hear about. These people only want to hear about the thrill you felt getting your medals handed to you and watching the flag go up and hearing 'The Star Spangled Banner' playin'.''

"Well, that wasn't as big a thrill as executing the back triple—"

"Lily! Now please stay with what I'm sayin'! I'm sayin' you're Cinderella come alive to these folks. Now try to act the way Cinderella acted just about the time the prince put the G.D. slipper on her G.D. foot!"

"Jeez, Ma, okay!"

"Just a year, Lily, of talking to a bunch of old farts at Rotary meetings and fat, rich ladies at the DAR. A year of being put up at the best hotels—it'll be a lot like Miami Beach . . . all those hotels—and nice meals and nice places to entertain our friend Rexhault when he comes to call."

Ah-ha.

"The man has no family, Lil. We're going to convince him that he wants us to be his family."

"We are?"

"Yes."

"His real family?"

"Yes."

"Like his wife and adopted daughter?"

"Oh, God, Lily!"

"Ma, remember in Vienna at the party where we met Sigmund Freud's daughter?"

"I remember."

"She asked me a ton of questions trying to see what made me tick?"

"Um-hmm."

"Until you said, 'The child is getting fatigued, Miss Freud.' "

"Lily, I remember."

"Ma, I believe you are the same as Miss Freud. You like getting inside people's heads without their really knowing what you're up to."

My mother laughed. "Well, that's true. Except I generally have to do it in three seconds, while that Miss Freud takes years!"

"You make it look easy, Ma."

"And you make diving look easy. That's why you're wearing these." She fingered the fake medals around my neck. They were not the real ones. The real ones weighed a ton. "I am so proud of you, Lily."

"Thanks, Ma."

"Now, sweet Lord, let's sneak into the powder room so I can fix this hair of mine."

I went right back to the party instead. You don't have to worry about your hair when it's in a tight braid, and wound around the crown of your head where some French maid has attached it with ten thousand pins.

In New York, before the tour started, Rexhault took my mother and me to the Stork Club for my sixteenth birthday. I had on my gold dress again. People stared at me. Rexhault asked me to dance, and I told him I didn't know how. He told me I had a lot of catching up to do. He danced with me anyway, and then a whole bunch of young fellows surrounded our table and asked me to dance, too. But my mother wouldn't permit it, thank God. She told them I wasn't allowed to dance with strangers. The place was full of girls dressed up like ladies, smoking cigarettes and drinking champagne. They were the debs, my mother said. They got to sit around at the Stork Club and El Morocco and go to parties. The debs stared at me. One finally came over. She had eyes like the dogs being walked on the promenade deck of the *Normandie*—wet and wishing someone who loved them would come back. She leaned over me and said, "Good for you, honey!"

The next day at the Plaza, not the Taft, my mother read Mr. Winchell's column aloud. She read,

"The Gilded Lily at the Stork Club . . . dancing the night away with the infamous Rexhault who kept New York wet when it wasn't meant to be dry . . . but wasn't it the Golden Girl's MOTHER, the wondrous Gertie Neelan, whom Mr. Rexhault had eyes for? . . . and what did our own glamour girl of the year, Eleanor ''Cookie'' Young, whisper in the Golden Girl's ear? . . . perhaps wished her luck on her upcoming world tour . . . nice to see a little girl without her mommy's rouge covering her pretty cheeks. . . ."

My mother put the newspaper down and chuckled. "What a feather or two for our caps, Lily. Just the thing Rexhault needs to see."

"Why, Ma?"

"Makes us all the more irresistible to him, Lily."

"He already likes us."

"Well, now, besides liking us, he'll be impressed with the talents we have which he hasn't seen yet and be satisfied that he had the right instincts."

What that meant I surely didn't know.

She went down to the Palm Court to meet some friends for coffee. I walked over to the New York Athletic Club to do some diving. At first, people just stared at me while I was doing my dives. They kept saying things like, "Wow! Wouldja lookit that!" Then they realized who I was. I think all the people in New York City found out where I was in about five minutes. It was Mr. Henderson from *The New York Times* who rescued me. His was the only face I recognized, and I asked him to please help me. He told everyone we had an appointment for an interview. In the taxi, I told him I couldn't give him an interview without my mother there or she'd kill me. He told me my mother would kill him, too.

"But this is no interview, Miss Neelan. I certainly intend to do an article on all that commotion back there, but no interview. However, I insist on giving you some fatherly advice, seeing as how you don't have a father, and seeing as I have three children. That is, if that's all right with you."

Here was a real pop. "Shoot."

"Don't stop diving, Lily. You are a wonder. Enjoy yourself. But be realistic about it. You can't do it without guaranteed privacy. You can't. You must accept this new turn your life has taken."

Well, of course, I already figured that out. But during my tour, there never was any privacy at all. Not until I got to New Haven. To Yale University, where I found a whole pack of friends a lot like the Fraley kids. And when I got there, I sent a note to Mr. Henderson of *The New York Times*. I wrote:

> *Dear Mr. Henderson,*
>   *Thank you for rescuing me. I am having my oak tree sent to you as a token of my appreciation. I hope that, besides three children, you have a yard. A yard to plant my oak tree.*
>
>   *Sincerely yours,*
>   *Lily Neelan.*

The tour was just the way my mother had described. She saw to that. She saw to everything. When I asked her a question, she answered as if she knew seconds before I asked her what it was I'd ask. She knew what I was going to ask when I asked her about speaking to the tour manager for the Olympic Committee about trying for an engagement in Florida.

My mother said, "I'm afraid that if we stopped for a few days in Miami Beach, it would make us too sad to think about continuing on with the tour."

"No, Ma, it would make us very happy."

"I mean, to spend a few days in Miami Beach and then have to up and leave again . . ."

"That wouldn't make me sad, either, because I know that once the tour ends, we'll go home again. A year is too long to be away! I want to go back to Florida, Ma." I got tears in my eyes. All I wanted was to sit by the crystal obelisk in the lobby of the Alhambra. On the *Normandie*, they have these beautiful crystal stanchions made by Mr. Lalique, all lit up from the inside out, and they reminded me so of our little obelisk.

"I can't go back, Lily."

"But it would just be for a few days. Ma, that's where champion divers are—in Florida. I'm sure Mr.—"

"Not ever. We can't go back ever."

"What?"

"We can't go back *ever*!"

"Why not?"

"Oh, if only I could make you understand. I try and I try, but you just don't get what our lives are all about."

I jumped up on the hotel bed. "That's right, I don't!" I stood on the bed as if it were the diving platform. "I miss Johnny Q. I want to see Eddie G. I want to show Eddie G all the stuff Mr. Modeen taught me. And now you're saying *ever*! What does *ever* mean?"

"Dammit, Lily, it's over. Over!"

"What's over?"

"Your childhood. Your diving. Miami Beach. It's time for us to start a brand-new life."

"What new life? Are you going to teach me to be a hooker, too?"

"Lily!"

"Well, what else can I do?"

She was sitting on the edge of the bed. She reached her hand up and took mine. "Please, Lily. Sit down here with me. I want you to be taken care of. You and me. We'll just be taken care of. Up till now, we've taken care of ourselves. Now, we're going to let someone else do the work. Once I know your life is secure, then you can go and do whatever you want."

"What I want is to go back to Miami Beach."

"Well, then, yes. When you're just a little older and I see to it that you have money that is your own, then you can go back."

"But how will you see to that?"

She got off the bed and stood up straight. I was now lying flat out on my stomach. "Lily, it's something I've worked toward just as hard as you've worked at diving. So after all that effort, how should you end up? A two-bit star in Billy Rose's Aquacades? Selling Firestone tires? I won't let that happen to you. I've realized that for us to be taken care of, we have to be part of a package."

"What package?"

"Rexhault's package."

"What does that mean?"

"Lily, think! I've explained this over and over."

"I know, I know. But just what does it mean to be a man's make-believe daughter?"

"I imagine the same as being a man's make-believe wife."

"Well, one thing I know. I ain't goin' back to Germany. I didn't like Berlin, if you want to know."

Her left eyebrow went up. "No one wants to go to Germany now, including Rexhault. A war's brewin' there. I know you heard all the talk of that."

"There's gonna be a war between Mr. Hitler and the Jews?"

She sighed. "Stay on the track, Lily. In Europe, there will be a war. But where we're goin' there won't be a war."

"Where's that?"

"I don't know yet."

"Ma!"

We looked at each other. No wonder she couldn't ever tell me what it was she was talking about. Half the time she didn't even know herself what she was talking about. We both started to laugh. We laughed and laughed. Then we hugged. Finally, she said, "We're goin' somewhere real nice, Lily. Somewhere where you can finish growing up and be safe. Then you can do what you want. It's just two years till you'll be eighteen. When you're eighteen, you can make all your own decisions, and in the meantime you will have wonderful memories to think back on. My one and only good memory I have is the first time I held you in my arms. You and me, Lily, we could keep doing this touring kind of stuff. But you hate it, and I'm gettin' real bored. Right now you have to trust me to make decisions for both of us."

"Ma?"

"Yes, Lily?"

"How come Johnny Q and Eddie G haven't answered my letters?"

"They can't."

"Why?"

"Because they know what's best for you."

I thought of Johnny Q's words about people you love not

being there when you need them. "You can't use people for crutches," I said, more to myself than to my mother.

"What's that, honey?"

"Nothin', Ma . . . Ma?"

"Yes, doll?"

"Do they get my letters?"

"Of course! And they love them. I'm sure they check the post office every day."

So I went off and wrote two letters, to Johnny Q and Eddie G. I told them I'd see them on my eighteenth birthday and how we'd celebrate and have the Putty Man get us all some chicken in a basket, and we'd have a picnic at Mr. Pancoast's park again, with all the Fraley kids, too. *P.S.*, I wrote, *Hello, all you Fraleys!*

Chapter 8

Rexhault came for us when we were in New Haven. We'd been on tour for six months. I agreed with my mother's opinion of our tour. It's fun to be treated like visiting royalty for a while, but after six months, it gets very boring. And it was only political once—when I was speaking to the ladies of the B'nai B'rith in Chicago. One lady asked me if I saw overt anti-Semitism in Germany. I said I sure did. I said I saw it in Florida, too. And I told them that if Mrs. Cloak could keep Jews out of her apartment building in the land of the free, who could tell what Mr. Hitler might do?

My mother stepped right up to the podium and said there would be no more questions as we had to get to our next engagement.

So when things got boring, my mother said, "We sure could use some sunshine and coconuts. I believe Rexhault has been left dangling long enough." That's when she called him.

I didn't bring up Miami Beach when she mentioned sunshine and coconuts. It wouldn't have done any good. But since we were in New Haven, I asked my mother if we could visit my granny. She said, "Granny's dead. You don't even remember Granny."

"I think I do."

"You are so sentimental."

"Haven't I got cousins or something?"

"I told you I had no brothers and sisters. How could you have cousins?"

"Maybe on my father's side."

One of her sighs. "Lily, neither I nor Granny knew who our fathers were, and neither do you know who yours is. And you never will."

"Oh, yeah. I forgot. Did you have a granny, Ma?"

"No, darling. All I ever had were cats."

"You must have asked Granny who her mother was."

"I guess I did. But her answers to my questions were never sound. She told me . . . what was it? Something like I was the governor of Louisiana's bastard, not the child of her dead husband."

"Whoa."

Rexhault arrived. He hugged my mother, and he gave me a very big hug, too. I hugged him back. I was surprised at how glad I was to see him again—to see someone who seemed now to be a long-lost member of what was the only family I'd ever had. First there was Johnny Q. Then there was Eddie G. Now, it seemed, here was Rexhault. I maybe didn't know my father, but I knew Rexhault.

As soon as I got him alone—after dinner in our suite while my mother got dressed to go partying—I asked him if he would help me. I used the word *help* without really thinking about it, but as soon as it crossed through the air between my lips and his ears, he reacted. He actually took a step back, as if he'd been swatted. I knew that he was afraid I was going to ask him something that didn't fit into his momentary life plan, like I wanted to start training for the next Olympics or something.

"Don't worry, Rexhault," I said. "It's nothing so serious." But to me it was very serious, and so I burst into tears. He passed me his handkerchief, which was as soft as talcum powder and as white. He breathed in a soft breath.

"What is it, Lily?"

"I want to find out where I came from, and my mother doesn't want me to find out. You're rich, and not only are you rich, but my mother likes you, to boot. You could talk my mother into letting me do this one thing."

He let the breath out, relieved. "Ah . . . well, this is not surprising about your mother. She wants two things in life, and she won't accept one without the other. She wants to have fun, and she wants to protect you."

"But it's not protecting me. It's the opposite. I want to *know*!"

"Yes, yes. You are a brave girl. I wish I were so brave. I only knew my mother, like you. But I don't want to know anything else. Why should I?"

"Aren't you curious?"

"Yes. But not brave."

"But how much did you learn before you decided it was enough? You know some things, I'll bet."

"When I knew that the truth about my mother would not match the image I had of her, I stopped asking. You are fortunate, actually, that your mother has at least given you some kind of honesty. But she herself wants to know nothing, and I understand that. We are aware of how terrible the truth can be. You have no such qualms. That's because of your mother's protection."

"Then before I get some qualms, I want to find out what's up. All my mother wants is smooth sailing on Easy Street. That's where you are, Rexhault. You're the king of Easy Street. But I don't like feeling . . . feeling missing."

"Missing?"

"Yes. I'm a missing person—kind of like I have amnesia. And so are you, Rexhault. How can you stand it?"

He just looked at me with curiosity.

I said, "I know, Rexhault, let's make a deal. Tell me what you know—even if it's not much—about where you came from, and we'll compare it to what I know, and we'll see who knows the most."

He shook his head, but was smiling. He said, "I am talking to a wall. However, I like deals. And if it will make you happy, good. But first I will make myself a little drink." He went over to the drink wagon. "Can I get you something?"

"Nope."

He raised an excellent eyebrow. "No, thank you is what you mean to say, Lily."

"No, thank you. Does a girl say 'no, thank you' even to her pop?"

"Certainly."

"Oh. I didn't know."

I was sitting on the sofa. He came over and sat across from me in a club chair and put his drink down. I waited, but stared at his face so he wouldn't think of some important phone call he had to make. He said, "My mother was a woman who decided, quite suddenly, to leave her wealthy family in Berlin in order to go riding on a Mississippi River steamer. So she did. Five years later, she came home, and she had me with her. I was two."

I waited, but he was actually finished.

"That's it?"

"Yes."

"Rexhault, had she gotten married?"

"She said she was a widow."

I slapped my knee. "That's exactly what my ma used to say. Isn't that a hoot?"

He didn't think that was a hoot at all. He kind of looked past me. I looked over my shoulder. Nothing was there. I looked back at Rexhault. He was still looking past me. I put two and two together.

"Why, then . . . Rexhault! Your mother must have been a . . ."

"Lily." He held up his hand.

"Well, I'll be snookered."

"I really don't care what she must have been. In Germany, with her family, she was just my mother. And a good one."

"Sure she was. So where is she?"

"She died during the flu epidemic a few years ago."

"Oh. I'm sorry."

"Thank you."

"God! Think of it. Here she was rich and on Easy Street . . . well, Easy Strasse . . . and she went off to take a boat ride. Isn't *anybody* happy on Easy Street?"

"Not if they don't know they're there. She was too young to know, and naturally, she'd never lived anywhere else."

(Another worm in the horseradish.) "She was the type of girl who needed an adventure before she settled down."

"Just like you, Rexhault, except you're a boy. Rexhault?"

"Yes?"

"I know you must have asked her who your father was. I just know it."

"She wouldn't tell me. However, when I reached my eighteenth birthday, she gave me access to a trust and to deeds to certain properties in America. In New Orleans and thereabouts. She told me the money and the land had been given to her by my father, and that now they were mine."

"So then you must have really asked her who your father was."

"Yes, I did. But she refused and told me it was her duty to protect me."

"Now there's another coincidence."

"What's a coincidence?" asked my mother.

She stood in the doorway to the bedrooms. She looked swell. She was wearing one of the new two-way stretches under her clothes that made a woman's body look like a smooth roadway with long curves. Oranges and grapefruit were not fashionable for a while back in the thirties. With me, they'd always be, because there was no way I'd zip myself into one of those foundation garments, even if it was designed by Gloriane herself. (My mother's were designed by her.) What did he know about having breasts squashed into a long, narrow tube?

Rexhault's natural reflexes had him on his feet. The look of pleasure on his face was as if he'd just completed a perfect inward pike without a splash. He went over and lifted her hand to his lips.

My mother said, "You two aren't keeping secrets from me, now are you?"

He answered, though my mother was looking directly at me. "Yes, my dear. We are. Secrets that will mean adventurous excursions here in New Haven."

Now, he kissed her cheek. Nuzzled it actually, like a pooch.

Hmmmmm. New rules for my mother. She knew there'd have to be a few, throwing in her chips with Rexhault, but here was a real surprise. The rules, it appeared, would have an effect on me. Until now, I had been solely her domain. She looked at Rexhault, and he winked at her. She smiled. The unexpected did give my mother great pleasure, and she had a lot of confidence that nothing she was in control of would get out of control.

They both kissed me good-bye.

The next morning, my mother put her head in my door very early. She said, "Your appointment today is for ten. Someone will be here to pick you up. So come on out and have breakfast with me."

I could hear room service clanking in with the dishes. I put on my robe and slippers and went out. I liked to eat before I did anything else. My mother liked to first bathe and dress in feathered peignoirs plus mules and narrow bands of colored silk tied around her hair. I sat down across from her and poured out my cornflakes.

"Today will be quite a lot of fun for you, Lily. I have agreed to an exhibition this afternoon. A private exhibition for the Yale diving team. Their coach and two of his boys will be here for you at ten. Then there will be a one o'clock luncheon with these Yale people. I will meet you—"

"Ma!" I was finally able to interrupt her without choking to death on my cornflakes. I'd swallowed most of my mouthful without chewing.

"Yes?" Her eyes twinkled.

"I get to do some real diving?"

"Yes, Lily."

I leaped up and threw my arms around her. "The coach is coming to get me?"

"Uh-hmm."

"Oh, God, I hope he's not like that Mr. Modeen. Who is he, Ma?"

"He's nothing like Mr. Modeen. He's much younger, for one thing. And he dived in the '32 games. You'll have a ton to talk about."

"He dived in the '32 games?"

"That's what I said, Lily."

"What's his name?"

"Now I have that somewhere . . ." She started fiddling with her appointment book. "Anyway, I've told this coach that you will be at the pool for just one hour, so don't you go get carried away. The luncheon will be very nice, and you'll need time to dry."

"I don't think anyone in Berlin was from Yale."

"That's right. Swimmers, but not divers. That's why their plea to me to allow you to dive for them was so heart-rending. They were quite adorable. Came right up to our table last night, handsomest boys I ever did see, and begged me. Of course, they didn't have to beg me. I'd have said yes right away because I knew you'd love it."

"Thanks Ma. Find the coach's name, Ma."

"I am looking!"

"I wonder if Eddie G ever mentioned this fella to me. He definitely competed in '32?"

"Yes. He won a bronze . . ." She was flipping pages.

"He did? All right! He's a champion."

"Gresham Young."

"Gresham Young! Whoa! He was the guy who tried to do a reverse one-half somersault with a two-and-a-half twist. He did it, too. That's why he lost. Mr. Modeen told me."

"He did it but lost? How's that?"

"Mr. Modeen said once when I wanted to try something nobody's done before that it makes the judges nervous. They've already decided what's impossible, so you don't want to show them up, see? And this Gresham Young . . ."

"Lily, sweetie, I have no idea what you're talking about."

"Anyway, he got hurt after. That's why he wasn't in Berlin."

"Whatever. Anyway, he'll be here shortly, so get yourself going."

"Okay, Ma."

"And Lily?"

"Yes, Ma?"

''Rexhault told me about the conversation he had with you.''

''Oh.''

''Lily, if you find out anything about me that you don't like, or if you find out anything you feel I should have told you but didn't, you won't hold it against me, now will you?''

''Of course I won't, Ma. Like what?''

She got wet eyes. ''Honey, if I ever kept things from you, it was because I love you so much. You're my girl. You're my family. You're all I ever had that was any good.''

''Aw, Ma.'' I went over to her, and we hugged.

''But Rexhault has made me see that you have your rights.''

''My rights? Why, Ma. That sounds downright political to me. Did you tell him to watch his step?''

She smacked my hind end. We laughed. I went and got dressed.

It took me a few minutes to put on my practice clothes, and to put a suit and towels in my bag. My mother would pick out my luncheon clothes and take them with her.

Back in the living room, I sat with her while she did her nails. I watched her.

''Ma?''

''Yes, baby.''

''Why don't you want to know?''

''I just don't.''

''But why? There's got to be a why.''

''I'm afraid.''

''Afraid of what? We've got Rexhault.''

She stopped to think. Think in flashes, the way she did, and she got so much thought out in that quick flash. ''Lily, you don't know how to be afraid. I could see that when you leaped off your platform like some old gooney bird. And that's because of me. I kept you from being afraid. Trouble is, maybe now you should learn to be. At least a little bit.''

''I'm afraid of some things.''

''Like?''

''Like boys.''

''Oh, Lily.'' She reached around my shoulders and gave

me a quick hug with her elbows while holding out her red, wet nails. "Boys aren't to be afraid of. It's not fear that you're feeling. What you are is . . . um . . . tentative. That's because you haven't had much chance to know a lot of boys. But you will."

"I will? When?"

"Why, in a few short minutes."

"Those won't be boys. Those are divers."

She laughed. This was trivial stuff to her.

"But, Ma, never mind boys. How about you try not to be afraid? Then me and you could go out with Rexhault and find out all about—"

She shoved her little brush back into its red bottle. "Because I choose to be afraid. I don't want to find anything out. I don't want to go back. And I won't. I've let Rexhault talk me into accepting your need to know because you . . . well, because it'll just be a story to you. To me, it will be pain. And suffering. Can you try to keep that in mind, Lily?"

"Okay, Ma. Ma?"

"Yesssss."

"This is the very last thing. What if I find out things that aren't awful? Can I tell you then?"

"If you find out we inherited a gold mine, or if we're the long-lost relatives of King George, then tell me."

We laughed, because we couldn't have known the portent of her silly words. Or how momentous the morning was going to be, since it was the morning I met Gresham Young.

There was a knock at the door, and the little porter announced Gresham Young and the co-captains of the Yale diving team. The co-captain fellows came tumbling into the room, very excited, and then stood there staring at me, blocking the way of their coach. From behind them, he cleared his throat, kindly. They excused themselves and then introduced themselves to me until finally Gresham Young got a chance to congratulate me and thank me for agreeing to come to the pool. Gresham Young made me think of the Rock of Gibraltar, though I'd never seen it.

Built to dive, too.

Chapter 9

So while I stood there, eyeball-to-eyeball, level with Gresham Young, suddenly I thought, Could this be my brother? Or a half-brother, or a cousin. A relative. Because I felt as if I were looking in a mirror, and if I had been a boy, this is what'd I'd have looked like, for sure. Except that his hair was as dark as mine was light, which meant he probably couldn't be my brother. *Oh, good, he's not my brother.* Then I felt sweat in my armpits and a little lurch as my stomach jumped up to where my heart was. Those were the feelings divers told me they had when they climbed the ladder. I never did. I did now. I was as silent as a cupboard. My mother said later that it was the first time in my life I'd met someone and wasn't wide-eyed and babbling within minutes.

This man standing in front of me was a coach? I couldn't believe it, I didn't know why.

Later, at lunch that day, my mother said, "Kinda short, isn't he?" She said that because though it was four hours since I'd met Gresham Young, I was still speechless. *Short* pulled me back.

"Short? Sew buttons, Ma. I like looking into a man's eyes without having to crane my neck."

"Good for you, Lily," she said. She liked Gresham, too. She said he was a nice boy. He was.

When Gresham and I left the hotel for the pool, the two Yale fellows kept scooting around me like puppies. They went on and on about what an honor it was to have me, and the great service I was doing the team, and what an inspiration I was. But I kept looking around them, taking quick glances at Gresham Young, and every time I did, his eyes would meet mine and he'd wink or he'd smile, a little embarrassed that his boys were making such fools of themselves. They really made fools of themselves when they realized we'd be driving to Yale in Rexhault's Bentley, driven by his chauffeur, Charles. I introduced Charles to Gresham and the boys, and while the boys asked Charles a million questions about the car's engine, I composed myself. I asked Gresham if we could stop at a sporting goods shop on the way to the pool. This request diverted the boys from Charles and the engine. They said:

"Oh, certainly, certainly."

Gresham Young said, "What exactly will you need, Miss Neelan?"

"Lily."

"Lily."

Nobody said anything, and I realized I hadn't answered the question. "Oh. Well, I need a bow and arrow, Mr. Young."

"Coach," said the Yale boys.

"Gresham," said Gresham Young. Then he said, "The physical-education plant at Yale would have everything a sporting goods store might carry."

I said, "I need a bow and arrow."

The Yale boys stared at me and made me feel like a Greek oracle who had spoken some profound thing. One said, "We have plenty of bows and arrows."

I said, "Oh, good."

The two of them grinned from ear to ear, they were so happy to please me. I heard Gresham chuckle. I did, too.

Charles said, "Directly to Yale, then?" Charles was such a good driver that he had been all prepared for the bow-and-arrow detour.

"Yes, Charles."

When the car stopped at Yale, the boys hopped out and immediately began a tug-of-war over my bag.

I said, "I think I'll just carry my own bag, before you two fellas rip it right down the middle."

That made them begin apologizing profusely, so Gresham Young said, "Dick, if you would carry Miss . . . Lily's things, and Gordon, if you would round up that bow and arrow . . ."

Then he took me by my elbow and ushered me into the Yale athletic building. We were still eyeball-to-eyeball, but I did get a few glimpses of Yale University with my peripheral vision. The school reminded me of Europe.

In the locker room, in my diving suit, I looked down at my body. My knees looked bony, my arms looked hairy, and my thighs looked good and naked. My nipples were sticking out, because I was shivering with fear. I was all alone in a giant locker room, afraid to go out.

Afraid, Ma. Now, I knew about afraid.

Instead of draping a towel around my neck, I put it over my shoulder to at least hide one nipple, and then I wrapped another towel around my waist, like Dorothy Lamour's sarong. I put my head up and marched out. If I had ever felt this nervous during competition, I would have never met that Mr. Hitler, for sure.

All the Yale boys were standing alongside the pool at attention. Gresham stood off to one side with his arms folded across his chest, his joints loose. He smiled at me. I smiled back. The fine dark hair on his chest looked like the waves of a sandbar. I didn't notice if the boys on the team had hair on their chests.

"Are you chilly?" asked Gresham Young.

"Yes," I lied. "I mean, I was, but now I'm getting warm. It was drafty in the locker room." I tossed the towels.

He said, "Gentlemen, our guest. Miss Lily Neelan."

They applauded. I said:

"Let's have a little swim," and I held my nose and jumped into the pool like Laurel or Hardy. So did they. Not Gresham Young. He stood there watching his boys having some fun, leaving it to me to know when they were relaxed enough to have a real practice. I climbed out of the pool.

The way my mother told me to do it, not like Laurel or Hardy.

For the next half hour, I dived, and for the half hour after that we all dived, and Gresham and I actually became a great coaching team—him talking about entries and elbows the way Mr. Modeen always did with me, and diving himself the way Eddie G would do when he didn't think the boys understood what I was saying. Then I imitated their mistakes, making the most godawful splashes, and this got them all to laughing—Gresham, too. When we were tired, I had one of the boys shoot the arrow up toward the ceiling, and we watched it come down into the water. And I talked about windup dolls, too.

Hey, I thought. I'm not such a bad coach.

When it was time to call it quits, I said to Gresham Young, "How'd I do?"

He said, "You were fine. I knew you'd be an inspiration to these fellas, but you were far more."

"Thank you."

"You're welcome. And thank you."

"You're welcome. You're a terrific coach, Mr. Young."

"Gresham. Thank you."

"You're welcome. So what kind of a name is Gresham?"

He smiled a tiny bit. "A family name."

"Oh."

A family. He had a family. It actually pained me to leave him. I could have stayed in that pool with Gresham Young for the rest of my life. And all those little puppies from Yale dancing around trying to please me was swell. I felt so good. A new kind of good, different from the good I felt when I dived well.

I would be in New Haven for three days. I asked Gresham if he wanted to come to the luncheon, but he said the team was leaving for Boston early the next morning. Those words were horrible to my ears. Maybe I'd never see him again! We shook hands when Charles came for me, and said good-bye. As soon as the car pulled off, I wept. When we got to where I had to meet my mother, Charles went and fetched her. I don't know what he told her, because she came running toward the car looking to find me dead. She threw open the door and fell in beside me, immediately pressing her palm to my forehead.

"My God, Lily, you must be finally coming down with chicken pox. You're all red and feverish."

I sniffed and swallowed down a lot of tears. "No, Ma. I'm not sick. I . . ."

"What, sweetie, what?"

"I'll never see Gresham Young again for as long as I live. I'll have to kill myself."

Now, she hugged me and squeezed me tight. When she pulled away to face me, she had a smile, but it was a sympathetic one, not a laughing-at-someone smile. "C'mon, Lily. Let's get dressed and have something to eat, and you'll feel better."

"No, I won't."

"Yes, you will. Besides, do you think that Gresham Young is the type of fella who likes girls who blubber?"

"Of course not."

"Well, then, wipe your nose, and let's get a move on."

My mother called him. She called and asked him to come by our hotel for dinner that evening. She told him how much I'd enjoyed working with him that day. He said he'd love to come. That is how any man would respond to a request from my mother.

She told me about the call while we were having a late-afternoon drink with Rexhault. I was astonished.

"Ma! How could you?"

She smiled. I threw myself into her arms. "Thanks, Ma."

"That's what mothers are for. Now, would you like to change, or . . . or maybe put on a little lipstick?"

"What for?"

She shook her head. "Never mind."

"You know, Ma, he saw me first in my gym clothes, and then when I was looking like a wet rat. If I get dolled up, it would probably be too much of a shock, I am so gorgeous."

Rexhault thought that was the most hilarious remark. My mother just gaped at me. All I knew was that I didn't want to impress Gresham with what I wasn't. I just wanted to see him once more before we had to leave New Haven, so that I could remember his face better. When I thought of Johnny Q's face, it seemed a little blurred.

We had dinner in the hotel dining room, and I watched as Rexhault and my mother and Gresham talked about the news of the day, which, of course, in 1937 was all bad. Then we went up to our suite, and Rexhault and my mother disappeared. Gresham and I sat on the sofa, and sipped fresh orange juice, all athletes' favorite drink, and I told him I especially loved orange juice because it reminded me of home. He asked me when I was going home, and I told him that I would be going to a new home, but I wasn't sure when and I wasn't sure where. I told him we hadn't decided. I told him my mother was my only family, and what do you know? He told me his parents were both dead. He looked as if he felt so bad that I changed the subject and asked him why he hadn't tried for the '36 team.

He told me about his injury. He showed me the long, jagged scar two inches above his ear under his hair where he'd caught the edge of the board. The thought of him being hurt and bleeding was terrible. I reached up and touched his scar while my eyes got wet. He said:

"Hey! I'm fine now. Just a little dented."

We both relaxed. I told him all about Eddie G, who I had enough sense to refer to as Edward Greene. He knew about Eddie G and Eddie, Jr. He was very sympathetic. Gresham certainly was a nice person. Then he had to go. I got tears welling up in my eyes again that I couldn't help. He became very concerned. I told him I thought I was coming down with chicken pox. He said:

"You need to make some friends, Lily. Your own age. You promise me you'll do that when this tour is over. Okay?"

"Yes," I said, but he was the only friend I wanted. "I wish I could go to school here. At Yale."

"I wish you could, too. But I'm sure where you're going there will be a university where you can enroll. Hopefully, with a diving team.'' He smiled. ''And you'll be able to show the coach what's what.''

I smiled, too. Then I said, ''I didn't even finish high school, though.''

I told him about Archie Williams. I said, ''Archie, who won the four hundred meters, told me to go to school. He went to the University of California. He has a degree in aeronautical engineering, because it's the closest he could come to flying an airplane. He wants to fly, and he can't because he's colored. So he told me to go to school and then I could do whatever I wanted to, because I have white skin. Isn't that sad?''

Gresham said yes, that it was very sad. Then he had an idea. He said he would speak with a professor friend of his about my going to college, because, he explained to me very kindly, if you're a special person, you don't have to finish high school to get a higher education.

Then I said, ''You know, Gresham, I'd be mobbed if I went to a university. I'll probably have to wait a while yet to go to school. Besides, wherever Rexhault takes my mother and me . . . well, knowing Rexhault, it could be a place where I won't even be able to speak the lingo.''

So he said in a bright voice, ''Then you can study the lingo. Learning a new language is great fun.''

''That's true.'' I certainly had enjoyed learning a little bit of French and German.

I walked with him to the door. I think he meant to kiss me good-bye in a brotherly way on the cheek, but somehow his mouth brushed mine very softly and quickly, and the warmth of his dry lips made me feel as though I'd just stepped into quicksand and was sinking. I *was* sinking, too. I had to grab hold of the little table by the door or I'd have been on the floor, for sure. He left. I went into my bedroom, and I cried all night long. I'd doze off and then wake up, and automatically I'd start crying.

In the morning, I snuck out to the sitting room, and fortunately there was some ice still in the bucket on the bar table, and I put the ice on my eyes. I had to face Rexhault for our planned excursion to find out what happened to my granny, and now I wasn't interested in doing any such thing, but I had to. And Rexhault was in the opposite mood I was in. He'd gone and gotten all enthusiastic about this adventure, and arrived all dressed in modern-day explorer clothes—a plaid cap and a big greatcoat and boots. He didn't even notice how unhappy I was, though my mother did. She kept acting really cheery about our going out to find Granny's house, which, of course, surprised Rexhault, which is why he didn't notice anything wrong with me. My mother gave us the address.

In front of the hotel, Charles was waiting in an open Daimler, which Rexhault had rented because he felt explorers needed something more adventurous than a little Bentley. The Daimler was full of lap robes made of fur. Rexhault had brought me a fringed scarf like his, which I wrapped around my neck. I said, "All we need now are goggles." He laughed. The expedition was starting out to be fun.

"Now here's the map, Lily. You're the navigator. Charles, I'll be driving today."

I thought Charles might be offended, but he just tipped his cap politely and disappeared.

It was freezing out. I bundled up in all the fur, and just left out my hands to hold up the map. Rexhault pointed out on the map where I'd lived until I was four years old. The map with the little dot on it helped push Gresham Young into the back part of my brain.

I tried to bring up to the front part of my brain my granny's face. But all I could see were cats. That one particular cat that had blue fur and knew how to talk. I was sure that the image was the remnant of a mixed-up dream. I heard the cat call out, "Fire, fire!"

I made a pretty good navigator. That, or—more likely—Rexhault was a natural explorer. If I said, I think we turn here, he would turn, and when I was wrong, Rexhault wouldn't get all annoyed or tsk-tsk me. He'd just say, "Let's turn this big Bozo around, then," and then he'd say to me, "I'm glad we made an error here, Lily. Why, look at the Italian stonework there around that house. The only place you can see such stonework is in Naples, Italy. In fact, the masons of Naples have pretty much stopped doing that kind of work, but here it remains an art, still practiced.''

Then, on we'd go until my next mistake.

Then, we found it. What was left of it. Pieces of what must have been a grand house stood in an overgrown, rock-strewn lot. The whole center of the house had burned away, and the two ends of the house might have held up a very big roof, but now they held up nothing. Tall, dried weeds from last summer blew in the cold wind above the black, burned rubble. They were strange-looking spindly weeds that must have liked whatever it was that the burnt wood had put into the soil. We walked around a little, but Rexhault was afraid to really explore. He said a wall could easily topple over on us. But that was all right with me. Nothing looked the least bit familiar. I got dejected.

"Rexhault, wouldn't you at least want to know if your mother was dead or alive? My mother has no proof Granny is dead, she just thinks it.''

"Yes, I would. Because my mother loved me. Maybe if you're a person whose mother didn't love you, you perhaps don't really care if she is dead or alive.''

"You don't believe that stuff about blood being thicker than water?''

"No, I don't. That's why I was never a very good German. Blood is blood, and it has nothing whatsoever to do with your mind or your heart.''

"I agree. Look at Johnny Q and Eddie G. Our blood's not the same, and I love them more than anybody. Just as much as my ma. And I even loved the Putty Man very much. And he was a Negro.''

"Now, do you know, Lily, what a German would ask? A German would ask, 'What if all of them were drowning—whom would you save first?' ''

"Well, I'd save my ma. We all would. Because she can't swim.''

He laughed. Rexhault's laugh would cheer up Scrooge himself.

"So what do we do now, Rexhault?''

"To get information, you go to the library.''

"Oh, good. A warm one, I hope."

"Yes, a warm one, and we will find out what it is we need to find out."

"I've never been to a library."

"Ah, Lily. Say it isn't so."

"It is. Well, actually, I did go once. With the Fraley kids. But the librarian wouldn't let me in, because my hair was wet. My hair was always wet when I was in Miami Beach." I felt my braid. "I'm still a little damp right now from diving yesterday."

I tried not to think of Gresham.

"Then maybe it's time to get your hair bobbed."

I didn't say anything, because I was too embarrassed to tell Rexhault that I secretly hoped to have Eddie G braid my hair one last time before I let my mother lop it off.

"Where's this library?" I asked, picking up the map.

"It's at the university. The most wonderful library in the world. The Sterling Library at Yale."

I felt a thrill. I was going back to Yale! I would walk where Gresham walked, and maybe even pick up a book that he'd read.

The librarian at the Sterling Library was not like the lady at Miami Beach. She was an explorer. She was called a research librarian. We followed her around and up and down miles of shelves filled with a million books. She dug around and sneaked peeks here and there. Then she put us at a table with a stack of books about old New Haven houses. She had an architecture encyclopedia so we could determine what year the house might have been built. We didn't have the heart to tell her we didn't care that much about the house— it was the owner we were interested in.

Then she went right ahead with the address we handed her—the tiniest piece of paper—and went off and looked at some books. She determined for us that the house was built in 1898, right at the beginning of the Spanish-American War. She tacked on that last bit because she couldn't help it, she was so full of information.

She went off and brought us a file that told what was in the *New Haven Journal-Courier* newspaper, and she went through it looking for information about fires. We just watched her. It was like watching a murder mystery at the movies. When she found what we were looking for, she didn't show us until she first scurried away to get the fire-department reports so we could see the official report on the fire as well as the newspaper account.

Rexhault said to me, "Librarians could run the world."

"Why don't they?"

"They have a poor picture of themselves. They don't know how extraordinary their powers are."

"You sound like Miss Anna Freud, Rexhault."

The librarian came back. She asked us if we'd found anything else in the newspaper file. We hadn't even looked. She looked. She found the exact clipping she needed from 1926. September. One week after my mother took me away. That's when the house burned down. There was an article about my granny, whose name was Jennie Neelan. And a picture. I didn't recognize her face. That's because it was an old mug shot. At some point, my granny had been arrested for something. The article said my granny was an eccentric and a hermit.

My granny had set the fire. She'd locked in all the cats first. They all burned. The firemen said the wailing was horrifying. One fireman who was interviewed said he was sure the house was full of babies. He also said there was a rumor that a child lived in the house. No remains of a child were found, however, said the fire chief. I stared at Rexhault, and he stared back.

Just before setting the fire, though, the article went on to say, she'd let her pet parrot out the window. There was a picture of a scared fireman with a parrot trapped in a dog catcher's net. I said:

"Why, that's the blue cat. The talking blue cat! No wonder he could talk. He was a parrot!"

The librarian said, "Why goodness, goodness me! That's our Rum Keg!"

Rexhault and I both said, "Who?"

She told us that my talking blue cat was a parrot named

Rum Keg. The librarian told us Rum Keg lived at Yale in a science building in the office of "our Professor Gallileo."

Rexhault and I said, "Who?"

"Professor Gallileo. But with a double *l* in the first syllable."

"Rexhault, can we go see the parrot?"

"Don't you first want to hear about your grandmother? If she owned the house? Or who owns it now? And maybe even where she came from?"

"I think I'm scared now, Rexhault. My granny burned down a house full of cats. She could have done it a week earlier, while I was still in it."

Rexhault reached over and put a hand on my shoulder. The librarian said, just as bright as a light bulb, "Our Professor Gallileo probably knows all there is to know about the poor woman. I know he did try to find an heir—you know, the bird's rightful owner."

"Shall we, Rexhault?"

"Well, I've always wanted to meet Gallileo."

We laughed. The librarian did, too, but no sound came out, as she had pressed her fingertips to her lips. Rexhault took her hand from her mouth, kissed the back of it, and said, "Thank you, madam. You have been an extraordinary help to us, and we are most grateful."

I thought the librarian's skin would melt right off her body. She sagged.

"Now, if you could direct us to the office of the professor with the parrot, we would be the more grateful."

It was difficult for her to come out of her semi-swoon, but she did, and she directed us. That Rexhault is a very handsome fellow. Not as handsome as Gresham Young, I thought, though Gresham isn't the type who would make anyone swoon. Wouldn't want to, whereas Rexhault loved that sort of thing. Of course, Gresham made me practically swoon, but not on purpose.

Chapter 10

Professor Gallileo was a skinny little Italian fellow from the Università Di Torino. We were lucky, as he was just back from his last lecture of the day. Rexhault introduced himself, and the professor looked at him as if he were dog doody. This amused Rexhault to no end, I could tell. Then Rexhault introduced me and said who I was, and this Italian professor went berserk with the thrill of meeting me and told me he was once a world-class cyclist and would have been in the Olympics except for the Great War. He kept saying, *"Che bella figlia, che bella figlia,"* and kissing his fingertips and was "honored, honored, honored" to be in the presence of such a successful Olympian.

We had to wait a long time for him to calm down before we could ask him about the parrot. Rexhault explained that the woman who had owned the parrot was my grandmother, and that I would love to see the bird. At that, Professor Gallileo clutched his hands to his chest and got tears in his eyes. They ran down his cheeks. He rolled his eyes to heaven. With great dramatic gestures, he explained that the parrot was probably dying. That he was easily a century old. That his beautiful feathers were losing their iridescence. His *"belle belle azzurre"* feathers. This magnificent parrot, most probably brought aboard a slave ship from Africa from some majestic rain forest a hundred years ago, was—*madre mia!*—dying.

Rexhault told me that the performance was no different from a great opera in Milan.

"Come, come, come, I take you to the bird now," the professor called as he led us through a maze of corridors and up and down staircases. At Yale, a lot of the buildings are really castles. I doubt you could be a student at Yale if you didn't have a good sense of direction.

In a lab with a lot of cages that had birds and mice in them, there was a big perch in the corner. Rum Keg was on it, staring at us.

"Do not worry," said Professor Gallileo. "His wings are clipped, so he won't fly at you."

The poor bird, I thought. Like having your legs broken, I bet. The professor spoke to him in Italian. I could tell that Rum Keg was confused. I looked into his face, and I remembered it. My imagination and the distortion of time had added whiskers and little pointed ears and blue fur instead of blue feathers, but I remembered him. I said, "Hiya, Rum Keg."

His head turned this way and that. He had a tiny bald spot where a person would have had his right ear. He took three steps to the right and three steps to the left. And then he screeched very loudly:

"LEE-LEE! LEE-LEE!"

At first, none of us said anything. Then Rexhault said, "But I can't believe this."

The professor jumped up and down, up and down, as the mice were doing in their cages. I put my arm up to the perch, and the bird jumped down, walked right up my arm onto my shoulder, and nuzzled his small head right into my ear.

"Hey Rum Keg," I said. "That tickles."

The professor stopped jumping and peered at the parrot. "The bird, he is crying!" Which set him to crying. I was beginning to think I never wanted to go to the opera in Milan. Then the professor straightened up, and said, "I am a fool. I must stop this. Come."

And he took us into a quiet little cubicle, where, instead of cages, there was a large silver and gold machine with tubes, and decorated with shining metal curlicues. He fiddled with it, and the smell of coffee filled the room. I've sipped coffee but never liked it. I knew I'd like this. I did.

The professor and Rexhault started talking about the *Fascisti*. Gallileo was very glad to hear how much Rexhault disliked Mussolini. They became friends. We drank the Italian coffee out of tiny little emerald-green cups. Every time I moved, to sit, to stir my coffee with dollbaby spoons, Rum Keg nestled closer. So I said:

"Professor, what if this bird has to do his duty?"

"I am begging your pardon?"

Rexhault translated into Italian, and the professor said, "Oh. Then he will do it. I will get you a towel. Oh, I am such a fool!"

He went out, came back with a towel, and slipped the towel under Rum Keg's feet on my shoulder. Rum Keg let him. Then the professor got a notebook. In it, he had recorded all the things Rum Keg had said. He also recorded the last dates the bird had said each thing. We could see by the dates that Rum Keg had stopped talking completely within six months after the fire.

"Of course, this 'Lee-Lee, Lee-Lee' is what he shouted at me over and over when he first arrived here. And whenever he was hungry, he'd say 'Rum Keg,' so I thought— Ah-ha! This is the little fellow's name. It was when he was dozing off that he would mumble his extensive vocabulary. As if he were trying to bring all his good memories back when he went to sleep. A remarkable bird. To think, he kept a memory of you in his small little head, and he hasn't seen you in twelve years. But anyway! Here are some of the things he repeated most often, though I doubt they'd mean anything to you, since you were so young when you lived in the same house with the parrot."

Professor Gallileo read from his list: Campeachy, Old Hickory, Five St. Philip Street, Mr. U. Sadly, he yelled, "Fire!" a lot. And he had a phrase that he repeated often. "We have a marque, we have a marque."

Rexhault and I stared at him. He smiled. He said, "Signorina, though none of this probably means anything to you, it means a great deal to me!'' Rum Keg lifted his head to peek at the professor.

"I have tracked down everything the parrot has said. Over a hundred words!'' The professor turned over a few pages of his notebook. "Now this Campeachy is actually Campêche, a once-thriving town on Galveston Island in the Gulf of Mexico, populated by pirates until it was ravaged and burned to the ground, fifty years ago. And Old Hickory was the name Andrew Jackson was called. He knew all about the Gulf of Mexico. He had to. To fight the great Battle of New Orleans. And this address the parrot refers to—five St. Philip Street. That is the address of the blacksmith shop owned and operated—as a front for clandestine activities—by the famous Jean Laffite!''

Rexhault said, "The pirate?''

"Ah-ha! Not exactly a pirate. Which is what our leetle birdie kept reminding me. He told me over and over that 'we have a marque.' A marque, you see, is a document issued by one country giving permission to private citizens to attack and steal the goods of a ship from an enemy country. And if you have a marque, you may kill and plunder like Long John Silver himself, but you are not a pirate. You are a privateer! Jean Laffite had such documents from several countries giving him authority to attack both Spanish and British ships. You see?''

I looked at Rexhault, and he looked at me. Professor Gallileo said:

"Never mind. Just let us all know that if Old Hickory had not the help of Jean Laffite and his valiant buccaneers, the British would have come right up the Mississippi. Of course, I don't believe it was Laffite's fighting abilities that helped General Jackson as much as it was the fact that Jean Laffite was one of the few people in New Orleans who could speak English! From Laffite, Jackson could figure out what was going on. And Laffite, actually, was more of a spy, and he controlled an entire spy system, and that is my hobby! I am the world's foremost authority on spying!

"But, no matter for that. What I am sure of is that this parrot belonged to the infamous privateer himself.''

"And how did the bird come to be in the possession of Lily's grandmother here in New Haven?" Rexhault asked.

"Ah-ha! This is the secret I have tried to unlock. In my searches of the pirate, I have found out oh-so-many things. One is that very late in life, in his eighties, while he was, of course, in hiding, as he had been for several decades, Laffite managed to find a safe haven. I don't believe he died years earlier, as historians would let us believe. Just because you're missing doesn't mean you're dead. Spies are, naturally, experts at losing themselves.

"Laffite in his later years had two children. Twins, possibly, but two boys, at any rate. One boy turned to the sporting life, and the second became a scoundrel. The sporting son disappeared, just as his father had, without a trace. The second son was shot dead. He had a wife, and he left her his only remembrance of his father—a rare blue African parrot. Laffite made his fortune in the slave markets.

"But anyway, the woman arrived in New Haven with the parrot and a child of her own. She called herself Jennie Neelan, perhaps because of the notoriety in the name Laffite. Who knows? Unfortunately, her property in New Haven was confiscated for nonpayment of taxes, and she had no bank accounts. So now, here is her granddaughter, who last year won two Olympic gold medals. A superb diver, just like her great-grandfather, the infamous Jean Laffite!"

Rexhault and I looked at each other again. He was speechless. I said, "Whoa, boy!"

Rum Keg screeched, "We have a marque! We have a marque!"

Professor Gallileo let out a scream of Italian and thumped his chest.

Finally, Rexhault said in a voice that was meant to humor the professor, "Lily, do you know what this means?"

"Yes, I do. It means that Rum Keg is my parrot. I get to keep him, isn't that so, Professor?"

" 'Tis true. You do!" shouted the professor.

Rum Keg then started shrieking, "Fire! Fire!"

Rexhault stood up. "Please, let us be calm. This bird will have a heart attack, and so will I." Rexhault has a very deep voice when he gives orders, and we all came to attention, even the parrot, who started his three steps to the right and three steps to the left across the back of my shoulders.

"Now, Lily," Rexhault said. "Try to pay attention. If what the professor says has some shred of truth . . . I mean, of course, if there is any proof . . ."

Professor Gallileo jumped up. "On my honor, sir . . ."

"No, no, Professor. I believe all that you say. What I mean is, if we can prove, *legally*, that Lily and her mother are descendants of Jean Laffite, there is sure to be an inheritance to be looked into."

The professor's eyebrows rose up together in a sad little tepee. "I am afraid his other son was given everything. And, as I said, the son, disappeared, too. Who knows where? Took up with a foreign woman, who sailed away with all his money. Now that part is based completely on rumor, I admit, but rumors are often the basis for truth."

Rexhault said, "Well, Professor, Lily and I set out on a little adventure, and now we will set out on a bigger one. It just happens that we are going to New Orleans in a few days on our way to . . . to . . . well, to what is a surprise for Lily. I planned to spend some days there, and actually, I am familiar with that city. Lily, now that we have tracked down your family, we will try to track down your fortune."

The professor gathered up all his notes. He packed them into his notebook, which was full of more notes. "Here, take this. This is all the evidence I've gathered on Jean Laffite. With the situation we have in the world now, I am busy turning to more practical matters. My business as a scientist, and my interest in historical detective work, will perhaps come in handy as we try to determine which direction this madman Hitler will proceed."

He thrust his ledgers at me and dashed out of the room. He came back in with a big sack.

"Here is Rum Keg's food. But he'll eat anything. And he loves to go out in the rain. But only in the summer, of course, so he doesn't catch a grippe. And in a few months, he will need his feathers clipped again by a veterinarian, so he can't fly. Unless you are going somewhere he can fly

without bothering anyone. Here, if I let him fly . . . ha-ha
. . . the university would send me back to Torino!'' He
laughed again, but then suddenly grew dark. ''Maybe I go
back anyway, and put some bombs under the big, fat fannies
of the *Fascisti*!''

Chapter 11

I may never have had a pet pooch before, but now I had something better. Rexhault and I thanked the professor, left with all his papers, the sackful of parrot food, and Rum Keg in a cozy box of towels, so he wouldn't freeze getting back to the hotel. Rexhault drove very fast. That was because Rum Keg was squawking like ten Indians on the warpath. As soon as we got through the hotel door, I let him out and he leaped right up on my shoulder, telling everyone around the desk that we had a marque, in case they didn't know. Rexhault and I marched right over to the elevators as if we were quite used to traveling with a parrot who decided to make up for years of silence. When we walked into the suite, my mother looked up from her crossword puzzle and said:

"Holy mackerel! Rum Keg!"

My mother knew Rum Keg. Then, in that moment of seeing her recognition of him, I knew that my mother knew a lot. All the stuff I knew nothing about. I'd always pictured her life as one horrible blot, but here was a particular.

"Ma, why didn't you ever tell me about Granny's bird?"

"Well, I don't know. What's to tell? He's just a real old bird, that's for sure."

"Where did Granny get him?"

"I have no idea."

"You never asked?"

"Good grief, Lily, you have a very thick head. If I'd

asked, she would have given me one of her crazy answers. Your granny and I did not carry on normal conversations. Of course, I keep telling you this, but it doesn't seem to sink in.''

''So what crazy answer might she have given you? Just to give me an example, Ma.''

''I don't know. Maybe that she brought him up from the swamp where she lived.''

She got up and came over to us. Rum Keg rolled his blue head out to her and squinted. He said in a soft little voice, ''Jennie.'' I think.

''Ma, did he say 'Jennie?' ''

''My God, he thinks I'm Ma Mère.''

''Who?''

''Your granny. That's what she had me call her.''

Now, Rexhault got into the picture. ''Ma Mère is French, Gert.''

''Well, she wasn't French. She was crazy.''

''But, Gert, she was something other than crazy, surely.''

''Then maybe she was French. One day she'd say she was from the swamp, and the next day the Britannia Islands or somesuch, and the next day Quintana Roo, wherever or whatever that is.''

She was getting agitated, so I said, ''Ma, can you believe this parrot remembered me? He said my name the second he saw me.''

''Well, he surely did love your cats.''

''Ma!''

''No, really, he loved to walk all about Granny's furniture with the cats. Has he meowed? He can imitate a cat real good. He can imitate a lot.'' She looked down at her perfect nails.

''Well, I still can't believe he recognized me after all this time, and said my name.''

''He should know your name. When I brought you home to your granny, he took one look at you and started squawking 'Lee-Lee' over and over. Scared the bejesus out of the cats—you crying and him screeching.''

I let that sink in. It sank in real deep. ''Ma?''

"Yes, honey?"

"When you brought me to my granny's, what was my name?"

"Agathea."

"Oh."

"But I called you Cuddles."

"You didn't call me Lily?"

She started to say something, but then looked over at Rexhault. He put his hand up to his forehead and rubbed. I said:

"Ma, I was named by a parrot?"

"Well . . . yes. Yes, you were."

"But my birth certificate said Lily."

"I know. But I had the birth certificate made up for you so you could go to school. Ski Ball Scavelli made it for me."

"But where is my real birth certificate? The one that says . . . Agathea on it?"

"Lily . . ."

"What?"

"Oh, Lily."

"What's the matter, Ma?"

"Honey, how many times do I have to tell you that I was never the make-believe mother you keep hoping I was?"

My mother went and sat back on the couch, and she put her face in her hands. Rexhault looked like something was hurting him. He said:

"Lily, your mother was so young . . . she didn't know anything. She didn't know enough to register your birth."

"What about the doctor?"

My mother stood up. Her arms were by her sides, and her fists were clenched. "No doctor, Lily. No husband, no father, no doctor, no mother, no anything. And I cannot stand to think about it, thank you very much." She ran to the bedroom door, but then turned before she went in. She had tears in her eyes.

"But you may keep the parrot." She slammed the door behind her.

I hoped and hoped Rexhault would say something first,

but he didn't. He was good and mad at me. So I said, "I keep forgetting. Poor Ma." Rexhault wanted to swat me, I could tell, so he still didn't say anything. "Maybe you could go tell her I'm sorry, Rexhault."

Now, he smiled sadly. "She knows you would not be cruel on purpose. But right now she must come to grips with having to remember again. Let's leave her alone and go out, and then we will come back in a little while and start over again, as if none of this conversation with your mother has happened."

We sat Rum Keg on his perch, filled up his little food and water dishes, and went out and had two drinks downstairs at the bar. Then we came back and knocked on the door. My mother threw open the door. She had on a new color lipstick and a big smile. She said, "Well, hello, you two. I was about to send out a search party."

We walked in. We all made believe that what had happened didn't happen. She said, "Wherever did you find that darling bird?"

Rexhault said, "We found it in a basket outside the door."

"Why, it's a foundling."

This went on and on between them, and it was sort of like watching a Broadway play. Then I got sick of it.

"Shoot," I said.

"Why, Lily, whatever is wrong?"

I sighed, sat down on the arm of her wing chair, reached for the box of bonbons on the table next to her crossword-puzzle book, picked one out, and put it in my mouth. Then I said, "I was named by an old parrot."

The phone rang. I picked it up and yelled hello at the person. It was Gresham Young.

He was calling me long-distance from Boston. I held onto his voice for dear life with both my hands. He said he wanted to wish me a safe journey to wherever it was I was going, and also that he hoped I didn't take his kiss the wrong way. Rexhault and my mother gave each other a look and sidled out of the room.

"Oh, no, Gresham," I said. "I took it the right way."

He said, "It's just that I was grateful to you and so full of admiration for what you'd accomplished. . . ."

I said, "Gresham, I took it the right way. How are you?"

"I'm fine. We finished ahead of Harvard."

"Congratulations!"

"Lily, I was going to write and apologize for being so forward, but . . ."

"Oh, I'm so glad you didn't do that. You have nothing to apologize for. It was a very nice kiss."

I heard him suck in his breath. "Listen, Lily, I don't think you told me exactly where it is you are going, and I would like to keep in touch with you."

"Well," I said, trying to seem self-assured, "wherever I'm going is to be a surprise to me from Rexhault. But I'll be there for only two years. When I'm eighteen, I'm going back to Miami Beach."

"Oh. In that case, before you go to Miami Beach, perhaps you could give me the address of where you'll be in the meantime. I mean, once the surprise is over."

"Oh, I will. You'll write to me?"

"Yes, and the boys, if that's all right."

"That would be wonderful."

"Perhaps I could write when you're in New Orleans."

"We'll only be there a few days. And I don't know where we'll be staying. But when I find everything out, I will write to you and send you my new address."

"I will be glad of that."

"I will be glad of that, too."

"I hope you will have a place to dive where you're going."

"Oh, I'm sure Rexhault will see to that."

"And a place to go to school."

"I hope so."

He didn't say anything.

"Are you still there, Gresham?"

"Yes, I am. You know, Lily, you are a funny girl."

"Thank you."

He laughed. Then he said, "I have to leave the line now."

"Good-bye."

"Wait! Lily?"

"Yes?"

"I look forward to receiving a letter from you."

"Good. Because you will."

"That's great. Well, good-bye, then, for now."

"Good-bye."

I hung up and went to the desk and took out some stationery to start a letter to Gresham. I told him about Professor Gallileo and Rum Keg and Jean Laffite. Then there was nothing else to tell him, so I put the letter aside to finish when I had more to tell him.

I went into my bedroom and put out all the lights and drew the draperies and sat on my bed. With my eyes wide open, I tried to see Gresham's face in the dark, and I tried to imagine his face coming toward me to kiss me. Then I closed my eyes, like when he kissed me. My heart thumped with the memory. I went to sleep a short time later, hugging my pillow.

In the middle of the night, twenty boys from Yale stood under my hotel window and sang "Moon over Miami." A group of singers called the Whiffenpoofs had come to serenade me. One of the Whiffenpoofs was a diver, but he had an injury, so he'd missed the trip to Boston. It wasn't very late at night, just a little after midnight, so all the guests, like me and Rum Keg, leaned out the windows, and we all enjoyed the singing very much. Pretty soon a lot of cars had pulled up, and all sorts of people had gathered on the street to listen, including my mother and Rexhault, who were just home from dancing. The Whiffenpoofs sang some more songs and ended with their, "We Are Poor Little Lambs Who Have Lost Our Way," and they sang that so beautifully and sadly that I could only think of how much I wished I could see Gresham Young. And didn't Rum Key chirp right along with the singing. Then they threw flowers up at me, but I was in the penthouse, and too far up to catch any. The guests on the lower floors caught the flowers and called up to me that they would send the flowers along, room service.

My mother looked up at me proudly, while Rexhault just shook his head. All the upturned faces reminded me of being up on the platform. I missed my diving. So I had to pull my head in and sit with Rum Keg nestled into my hair. I cried. My mother and Rexhault soon came in.

"Why am I so sad?" I asked my mother. "This has been such a wonderful day."

She said, "You're not sad, you're in love."

"Yes, I am in love. Shouldn't I be happy, then?"

She knelt beside me. "No, dolly. Only in the movies are people happy when they fall in love."

"Well, that's no good."

Rexhault said, "But it's not a sadness caused by pain now, Lily, is it? It's a sadness caused by a sweet deprivation. A longing. So you have to console yourself with looking forward to seeing the young man again, because when you do, then you won't be sad anymore."

"Then she'll be miserable."

"Now, Gert."

My mother said to me, "Listen, Lily, if you don't want to be miserable, remember that when you see Gresham Young again, you'll feel like Cinderella for a few seconds. That will be a swell feeling. But that'll go away, and you'll have to face all the problems that come with being in love."

Rexhault sighed, "What your mother is saying, Lily, is that you must enjoy the lovely moments so that you'll have the strength to handle the bad ones."

"And why not tell her that for every lovely moment there are a thousand bad ones?"

I said, "Ma, I never see you and Rexhault having any bad moments."

"Well, we do. But not too many. That's because, between the two of us, we've been playing at this game for fifty years. You've been playing it for one day. You've a lot to learn."

"I don't believe that if I see Gresham again, there will be any bad moments. He's so nice."

"Nice has nothing to do with it. Naturally, I don't expect you to believe what I'm saying, but I have to say it so that when I prove right, you won't be mad at me for not warning you. Now, go blow a kiss to all those boys freezing down there on the sidewalk so that they can go back to school and get some sleep. And please put that parrot back on his perch before he tries to fly out the window.''

Rum Keg would never do such a thing, because he knew he couldn't fly. I put him on his perch, and he hid his little head under his wing right away, he was so tuckered out.

I went to the window. The Whiffenpoofs were all there. I waved, because blowing kisses seemed foolish. They cheered and then they left, and everybody went to bed.

Chapter 12

We rode the train from New Haven to New Orleans in Rexhault's private car. Rum Keg loved it. The car was furnished like a room in a Bavarian castle, except the carpet was long and skinny. On the Pullman, Rexhault informed us that he was born in New Orleans. I told my mother that Rexhault didn't know who his father was, either.

"I know, honey. Another missing man." My mother laughed. Rexhault smiled, but he didn't laugh.

Later, while my mother napped, I asked Rexhault if we should go on a second hunt while we were taking care of this Laffite business. A second hunt to find out who *his* father was.

"I'd like to do that, yes," he said. I was surprised, but then I saw that twinkle in his eye. "Who knows? We might find another parrot."

Rexhault and I didn't set much store on Professor Gallileo's theory about my being the great-granddaughter of Jean Laffite. But it was an adventurous story all the same, and Rexhault so loved adventure. Since he was in a good mood, I asked him, "So what do you think, Rexhault? Was your mother a prostitute, too?"

He looked out the window at North Carolina. I did, too. We were chugging slowly past a military base. The soldiers reminded me of the Whiffenpoofs. So I thought out loud. "Gresham Young's parents are dead. I hope before they died they were really his parents."

''I'm sorry, Lily, what was that?''

''Oh . . . I was just hoping that you could find out who your father was, even if he wasn't your official father. I'll never find out about mine, not ever, I can tell.''

''You know, Lily, I think I would like to find out who my father was, actually. But I want you to know that I did ask my mother once. That question. Who he was.''

''Hey, no kidding. What'd she say?''

''She said . . . now let me find the correct English for this . . . she said he was an old coot.''

''An old coot?''

''Yes.''

''That's all?''

''Yes. And whoever this old coot was, he sent my mother back to Germany with a very generous amount of money and several land deeds, which she has gifted me with. Some of the deeds were very simple ones, but now I must find out just exactly what belongs to me.''

''In New Orleans?''

''Yes. The deeds are for land in the area.''

''So that was all she said? About your father?''

''Your persistence is remarkable. She also said he was dead.''

''Oh. Where's he buried?''

''He's not.''

''Beg your pardon?''

''He's buried at sea.''

''Oh. I wouldn't like to be buried at sea.''

''Nor I. Or worse, I would dislike even more to be the gravedigger for that sort of burial.''

''Hah! You're a card, Rexhault.''

Rexhault and I laughed. He was pleased with himself whenever he made a joke in his second language.

In the city of New Orleans, some people speak English. But a lot sure don't. People speak French and Spanish and a mixture of everything called Creole, and then there are some real strange birds who are Cajuns, and I don't know what it was they were speaking. And there were Negroes and Indians, too, and they had accents, but I could understand them. Of all those kinds of people in New Orleans, the Negroes were the most fun. That's because they were the fellows who had invented jazz, and jazz was still going strong in New Orleans.

Rexhault was busy with his business the first few days in New Orleans, but promised me we would begin our search as soon as his affairs were in order, and maybe his affairs—these land deeds of his—would give him some clues to help toward the detective work we'd be doing. Procrastinating was all right with me, because I was very tired those first few days. I was used to going to bed early, but in New Orleans I was up most of the night along with everybody else in the city, it seemed, going to Bourbon Street to hear Louis Armstrong and Bunk Johnson's band, and we got to hear Cleanhead Vinson play the sax and Billie Holiday sing with the Duke. My mother kept saying, "I could stay in this town for the rest of my life with no trouble."

Besides staying up until all hours, the people in New Orleans especially loved to eat. My mother has a very big appetite. She'd dig into big bowls of gumbo or jambalaya or rapie pie, and eat plateloads of ugly green vegetables that looked like people's insides. Green intestines. Give me cornflakes, any day. My mother told me I was just lovesick and couldn't eat and that I should try to be lovesick in places where the food is terrible, not in New Orleans.

"Not being able to eat," she told me, "is just one of the many difficulties connected with love that I spoke of earlier, Lily."

On our third night, we came in to our hotel at 4:00 A.M., and I was beginning to feel disordered. That's because no matter what time I get to bed, I'm up at the crack of dawn, ready to go dive. I surely loved listening to the jazz men, but I was so tired, I was beginning to feel blue. That third night when we walked into the suite, my mother said, "Well, well, well, something for you, Lily."

On the little table next to the door was a letter from Gresham. My heart soared. The envelope was addressed to me at our New Haven hotel and Gresham had written in big red letters, ''Please forward to Addressee's New Orleans hotel.'' The postmark was Boston.

I ran into my room, propped myself up on all my pillows, and settled in to read the letter. Besides the story of Rum Keg, in my letter to Gresham I had also told him how the Whiffenpoofs had serenaded me. So in his letter he told me that divers shouldn't be out singing in the dead of night— especially one who's supposed to be nursing an injury. He said that particular fellow would be doing a few extra laps up and down the pool the minute he got back to New Haven. He also told me that the team's inspired victory over Harvard was due largely to me.

Then he told me how much he enjoyed my letter, since as a student at Yale he had studied with Professor Gallileo and had spent many happy hours in the company of Rum Keg. I read that part of the letter aloud to Rum Keg. Rum Keg said, ''We have a marque, we have a marque, squawk, squawk.'' Gresham's letter was like talking. I could even hear the sound of his voice saying the words.

He ended his letter by telling me that for some reason he found himself thinking of me quite a lot, and hoped I wouldn't be offended, since he was so much older than I was.

So I wrote back and told him that my mother's beau, Rexhault, was *ten years* older than she was, so there was really no offense, ''not that you are a beau, Gresham, of course.'' And I mentioned that I had been thinking of him a lot, too. Then, very quickly, I told him about reading the part of his letter about Rum Keg to Rum Keg and what Rum Keg said. And I told him what a marque was, in case he didn't know. And at the end of my letter, I told him that Rexhault had promised me that we would get to wherever we were going within a week and that I would let him know that address as soon as I could, and that in the meantime Rexhault and I would be trying to find out who Rexhault's father was. I asked Gresham Young if he had a normal, regular family, but apologized if that was too personal a question. I told him I hoped he did. In the P.S., I asked him why he was a diving coach if he'd studied science at Yale. I asked him why he wasn't a scientist.

Then I kissed the letter good-bye and mailed it.

In New Orleans, I was able to get my mind off Gresham Young for two reasons: one, I knew I wouldn't hear from him again until we reached our destination, wherever that was; and two, Rexhault became very intent on finding out who his father was. Children don't really think things all the way through when they're children, so that when they get to be adults, they're amazed at themselves for the way they'd always accepted other people's wanting them to put a stop to their curiosity. Rexhault's mother had stopped him with the words "Your father was an old coot." And Rexhault couldn't believe that he didn't say, "Mother, what was the old coot's name?"

Rexhault had done a lot of illegal things in his life, mostly smuggling. Consequently, he was very clever at hiding from people. Now, instead of being the source of what it was the authorities were searching for, he became the searcher. He found his new role very satisfying, because he was so naturally good at it. And besides that, he was such a commander kind of person that he was able to order people to do his searching for him, usually by charming them the way he did the librarian at the Sterling Library at Yale.

He and I drove about New Orleans, our first stop the famous Laffite blacksmith shop that Rum Keg knew the address of—5 St. Philip Street. Rexhault said it was actually just a tourist trap based on a story someone made up. He doubted the pirate actually owned it. He told me that if I were ever to visit Lincoln's log cabin, I could be sure that it wasn't authentic. And if I ever went to the Lebanon and somebody showed me a piece of Jesus' cross, I shouldn't expect any kind of a miracle to happen.

So I said, "But it's the same address that Rum Keg said to the professor."

He said, "Lily, I have a feeling that someone, probably your grandmother, taught the bird to say all those things so that people would think she did have a connection with Jean Laffite, but I doubt very much that Professor Gallileo's the-

ory about a lost son has anything to do with your grandmother.''

''I doubt the same thing.''

''I thought so. But you didn't say.''

''Too much fun to throw a damper on it.''

''Lily, you've a head on your shoulders, thank God.''

We peeked around the dank, dark, deserted, and peeling
blacksmith shop, and gave an old Negro man a dollar to
show us around. We explained we had a parrot that someone believed once belonged to Jean Laffite. The old man
thought that was very funny, but he had a good time taking
us into the shop's even danker little cellar and showing us
a secret escape hatch. So we laughed at that, and he swore
that it was used all the time and led to a closed-up tunnel.
When the tour ended, we thanked him very much for trou-
bling with us. Rexhault's generosity and our gratitude and
his not really wanting to see us go caused him to tell us that
he knew the grandsons of some of Laffite's men. He told us
he'd sure be glad to bring them around to meet us and our
parrot, and that we'd more than likely enjoy listening to the
old pirate stories, and that we'd all have quite a lot of fun
if the Cajun beer flowed free.

Then Rexhault brightened up just the way my mother does
when someone mentions a party. He told the Negro man to
bring his pals around to our hotel at eight o'clock, and we'd
have dinner in the private banquet room. The Negro man
said, '' 'Scuse me, sir, but if it's a Cajun feast you-all might
be interested in, then you meet all of us at backside of the
Vieux Carré in the Marigny houses 'stead of your hotel,
though it must have some handsome fine food, I'm sure. Be
more comfort. House number *trente*.''

Rexhault agreed. We went back and told my mother, who
immediately started planning what she'd wear to dazzle the
pirates' grandsons. I was a little worried about bringing
Rum Keg along, but it was a warm day, and if Rum Keg
really had belonged to pirates, he'd have one swell time with
these fellows for sure.

Rexhault told us that the Marigny houses were rows of
shacks built for slave women who were mistresses to several

men each. They had two rooms, one for business and one for all the mulatto children.

My mother listened to Rexhault very carefully while he told us about the Marigny houses. Then she went back to rummaging for her jade beads.

Chapter 13

As we got out of the taxi, I heard a yell, "They're here, Coranna!"

Rexhault held the shack door for my mother and me, and for the first time in a long time, our entrance took a backseat to someone else's. To Rum Keg's. There were twelve men sitting at a big wooden table, and they all twelve leaped to their feet and shouted, "Rum Keg" in such exact unison that they reminded me of the Whiffenpoofs. I lost what good manners I'd been taught, and amid the squawking and exclaiming, I shouted loud enough to disrupt the disruption.

"How could you fellas recognize this here parrot?"

Like most people, I thought a parrot was a parrot. Wrong. They started explaining to me all at once about his blue head, and you only see that kind of sapphire-blue feather in a parrot from Guinea in Africa, and they'd never heard of a single one of those Guinea parrots surviving the trip by slaver except for Rum Keg. And these twelve old men acted as if they were seeing a long-lost loved one, and their faces went from surprise to joy to great nostalgic sadness. Fortunately, that's when my mother's presence made itself felt.

She sailed around the table, trailing chiffon and perfume and holding her cigarette holder at a chic angle. Then the men started whipping off their little caps and holding them to their chests while my mother's sweet voice scolded, "Now you gentlemen please do sit down and cheer up while I direct myself right on over here to the middle of this . . .

uh . . . bench so that I am completely and totally surrounded by masculine pulchritude.'' My mother must have been taken by some Mae West movie to remember a line like that. The men stood like wooden Indians, staring at her as she slid down the bench, sat upon it as if she were settling herself onto a velvet-cushioned throne rather than a slab of wood that could leave slivers in her hind end, for sure. I climbed over the bench opposite her on the other side of the table, sat down, and petted Rum Keg's head so he'd quit his racket. I couldn't believe it. Rum Keg's old pals. My granny may not have been Jean Laffite's kin, but she sure must have managed to get hold of his parrot. Rexhault couldn't believe it either, but being Rexhault, he had regained his composure and his presence was immediately felt by the men who started bowing to him as if he were King George.

"Sit, sit, sit, gentlemen, and call for that wonderful New Orleans brew you promised me."

The word *brew* was all they needed, and they clambered onto the two long benches and out came a big Negro lady who threw a length of red oilcloth down the table with one hand while she held a tray over her head with the other. The tray held fifteen mugs of homemade brown beer that might have been so many cotton balls, the way she swung it down onto the table. Rexhault took her hand, kissed it, and asked her if she might have a chair for him. She laughed and laughed and said, "One chair comin' right along, suh!"

Then, out came this little tiny black man dragging a huge armchair, which the lady whipped away from him and set at the end of the long table. Rexhault said, "Thank you, madam," and sat. Rexhault wouldn't know how to go about sitting on a bench, and he wasn't ashamed to admit it, either. He took the last mug of beer and raised it in a salute. So did everyone else. Then they started guzzling. I took a sip of mine, hoping it wouldn't taste like bitter medicine, and it surely didn't. It was dark brown beer, and the thick white head spread onto my top lip liked whipped cream. Everybody's Adam's apples were going up and down, up and down, but it was my mother who was first to empty her mug and smack it down on the table. The men were very proud of her, and by then two more trays of beers had already arrived, one at either end of the table.

Then there came a great smell of food, a kind of smell that I knew right then you'd only get in New Orleans and nowhere else, and the smell immediately made you feel starved to death, as if you hadn't eaten in weeks. The door opened, and a big cloud of steam blew in from the back room, followed by three little Negro boys holding out great platters of red-shelled water animals. They looked like baby Maine lobsters, and each and every one of them stared up at me with their little eyes. I wasn't a big seafood fan, but I just watched my mother and did what she did, which was to peel the shells right off these animals—each one was about six inches long—and start dipping them into little bowls of goo. They were very tasty, I had to admit. Or maybe it was the goo that was tasty, I didn't know, but soon the goo was covering my chin and slathering on down my arms, and I kept right on being a pig just like everyone else, though my mother and Rexhault stayed clean throughout the whole operation.

One little Negro boy dug into his shirt and pulled out a harmonica. He started playing a tune, while the other two danced some kind of a jig with each other, dancing around and having a gay old time. I felt as if I had landed in some foreign country. New Orleans is more foreign than France, though not Germany—all those uniforms. Long after I'd had my fill of those lobster things, about the time everyone was digging into the tenth platter or so, I just wiped my hands and mouth with one of the big wet towels that kept getting passed around and leaned back and watched the men who were, by now, up to their elbows in empty shells and chewed, twiggy legs.

Every man was easily over seventy years old, and a couple looked like pirates. But mostly they looked like everyday old men. Some were blond and blue-eyed and some were black as midnight, and then there were some West Indian-looking types—coffee-colored. They said their names as they took turns talking, and their names were so strange that I remembered who was who quite easily. They were Mr. Gambi and Mr. Beluche and something like Mr. Chiaghazzi and Mr. You, who said, "I am Mr. You, Y-O-U, the grandson of Dominique You, Laffite's personal bodyguard." I remembered Professor Gallileo saying Rum Keg mentioned a Mr. U. Well, here was the man's grandson. Whoa, boy. The two big blond fellows were Mr. Jellness and Mr. Jorness. The other six fellows were happier to drink than talk, so they drank.

Rexhault started the talkers off by saying, "Well, then, gentlemen, what really happened to Jean Laffite?"

And so we got a full history of the pirates of Barataria Bay, which is where the Mississippi meets the Gulf of Mexico. The men claimed their granddaddies were all in Laffite's gang. They said how Laffite had no longer been welcome in New Orleans after the war since he'd gone back to his old ways while America was trying to become a civilized country, and settled himself off the Texas coast on Galveston Island. He set up a big pirate community where all buccaneers and pirates and privateers were welcome. It actually became a city-sized town and it was called Campêche (which these old men pronounced Campeachy, the way Rum Keg did). Every time the name Campêche came up, Rum Keg would pace on my shoulder. He'd quieted down, but he never stopped pacing. Mr. You said thousands of men came with their families to live on the island, but of course they continued to make their livelihood by going out and attacking ships and plundering.

All this was such an embarrassment to Governor Clayton of Louisiana that he decided to get rid of Laffite once and for all by attacking Campêche. Mr. Gambi said that Clayton wanted an excuse to get Laffite because Laffite had once spooned with Mrs. Clayton. But Jean Laffite heard of the plan, and when the governor's army arrived at the island, the whole town of Campêche was on fire and not a pirate was to be found. And Jean Laffite was never to be heard from again. *Except* by his closest men, many of whom stayed with him. Now here was where the men started to differ with each other. They argued that Laffite went to Cuba or Key West or Venezuela or Cartagena or Quintana Roo.

My mother chimed in, ''Quintana Roo?''

''Damn right, ma'am,'' said Mr. Jellness, ''but Laffite wouldn't go there with all those Spaniolis.''

Mr. You insisted the hardest that where he really went was to one of the Dry Tortugas; said that Andrew Jackson felt bad about the burning of Campêche and saw to it that the U.S. government gifted Laffite with one of the Tortugas. Several of the men laughed at this.

''Hell. He couldn't go to them Tortugas.''

''Why not?''

''Why you think they called Dry, you dumb boy?''

''Because they got no damn water.''

''Boy ain't wrong. They got no water.''

But Mr. You begged to differ. ''My daddy was there. He said it had water.''

''Your daddy a damn liar.''

''My daddy no damn liar.''

''He ain't wrong! His daddy no damn liar, I'll vouch for that. 'Cuz his daddy was the son of a real pirate, and pirates lie, but not to each other. And hell, my daddy and his daddy was good friends. And my own daddy did say Mr. Laffite found a place that had no water, but that he went there anyway.''

I got a little sad listening to all the talk about daddies. Until I happened to look at Rexhault. His eyes were bulging out of his head.

Mr. You said, ''That's because there *was* water. On one of them Tortugas was an underground river, but it didn't cause no sinkhole, so it never be seen. But Laffite found it, and he found cisterns, too, filled with water. Whole caves filled with water—damn sweet water! Nobody know'd except Laffite and his brother and my granddaddy and Laffite's woman,'' said Mr. You.

''Anyway, Laffite let my granddaddy hide out on that key with him. The dry one that actually had full innards of water. Loggerhead, it was called. I remember that now, I do.''

Mr. Gambi said, ''Now, hell, if there's such a key—one

with a secret supply of water—how come nobody's living there now?''

"Well, when Laffite died, he had those cisterns covered up. He was a strange man, Jean Laffite, and he liked the idea that no one would know what happened to him—where he died and where he was buried. But my granddaddy knew about it because Laffite hid him there many a time. But my granddaddy didn't call it Loggerhead Key, that place. He didn't want to give anybody any clues about where to find Laffite.''

Now I could see that Rexhault was acting more and more strangled. My mother asked, "You okay down there, honey?'' He nodded, but he wasn't okay. He'd had too much to drink and was getting a little nervous that this wasn't all hooey after all. The men kept talking. Mr. You said, "So here's what else I know. Laffite had two sons.''

I piped up, "Twins.''

Mr. Jellness said, "I never heard those boys was twins.''

"They wasn't,'' said Mr. Gambi.

"That's what Dr. Gallileo thought,'' I said.

They all looked at me as if I were a toad.

"Well, hell, I never met a doctor yet who wasn't a dumbbell.''

"You ain't wrong there, old friend.''

Then they started a big argument about whether the sons might have been twins and whether one was a girl, and it took a long time before the pirates' grandsons resolved that there were two boys and they definitely weren't twins.

"Anyhow,'' said Mr. Gambi, "one ran away with a crazy woman.''

Mr. Jorness said, "I know that for a fact myself.'Cuz that crazy woman shot that Laffite boy right in the head once he done her wrong. She wasn't crazy till then. He made her crazy. He was no good. Her name was Jennie, weren't it?''

"You ain't wrong.''

I must have made some sort of noise, because they all shut up and looked back at me. I said, "My granny was a murderer?''

Everybody was drunk as skunks. They all stared at me.

They never wondered how I came to have the parrot that they remembered as small boys. Now, they knew. Mr. You said to me:

"Now hell, little girl, don't you worry none about that. Your granny shot that Laffite boy who was a greedy summabitch in self-defense."

He made that up to make me feel better, I could tell.

Rexhault said quietly, "What about the other son?"

Mr. Gambi said, "He was a gambler. Married a riverboat dolly, then had to disappear because of debt. Left the dolly everything in her name. He was a good one, that boy. Not like his no-count brother." (A glance toward me.) "Never saw him again, either. Probably went back to that Loggerhead Key, just like his daddy did. Nothin' out there but peace, and sometimes a man just wants peace."

Rexhault said, "Did anyone ever hear who . . . um . . . who that riverboat dolly was?"

"It were a damn foreign woman, I believe."

"You ain't wrong. She was a foreign woman."

"Damn foreign."

Rexhault said, "What country was she from?"

One said, "Belgique," one said she was a Spanioli, and one said, "Allemagny."

I watched my mother's eyes and Rexhault's eyes lock. This was how my mother saved him from choking to death, because he couldn't take any more once he'd heard "Allemagny." She held on to him with her eyes while Mr. You finished the conversation with, "Yessiree, one son got Laffite's fortune and gave most of it to his woman, and the other son did his wife wrong and got kilt for it. But Laffite died a long, long time before any of that, so he didn't much care."

Then the men noticed the faces of my mother and Rexhault and politely went back to some chatter that had nothing to do with anything and started drinking loads more of beer. I said, "Allemagny is Germany, I know, but, shoot, Rexhault, maybe she was a Spanioli after all."

My mother's and Rexhault's gazes unlocked, drifted over toward me, drifted back to each other, and they both at the exact same time burst out laughing. They laughed so hard that my mother was holding on to her sides one minute and banging her fist on the table another, and Rexhault, of all things, had to dab at his eyes with his immaculate hankie. All I need is to see laughing and I start to laugh, too, because who wants to miss out on a joke, and then the pirates' grandsons joined in, and the little Negro boys really started dancing up a storm, and I swear the walls of the room began to shake. We laughed till we couldn't anymore, and the room became full of exhausted sighs and my mother said to me:

"Lily, according to these gentlemen, His Excellency Albert Rexhault is the family you have always wanted. Your cousin, I would have to say, though once removed. Why, we are all cousins! Oh, Rexhault, honey, isn't that just high hat?"

"It is, it is," said Rexhault. "But I do believe, Gert, that I will have to hire you and Lily a couple of lawyers, because half of what I got from my mother, of course, is rightfully yours."

"I hope you'll hire damned good lawyers, Rexhault," my mother said, smirking.

"That I promise."

I said, "Ma, set me straight. Exactly what has happened here?"

The pirate offspring were all ears, and their eyes were as big as saucers. She said, "Lily, imagine that. It could just be that Rexhault's daddy and your granddaddy were brothers! Could be that they were the sons of the famous pirate . . . excuse me, privateer, Jean Laffite." Then she turned to the pirate offspring, bringing every one of them into her look, like a good teacher does with forty grammar-schoolers. She said, "This little girl is the grandchild of the crazy woman who shot Laffite's son. And this gentleman is the son of the woman from Allemagny. Which makes us all cousins. Kissin' cousins, at that."

"Well, I'll be damned," said Mr. You.

This was a very exciting thing to happen to the men. They'd never had excitement before, only heard about it.

They were practically berserk with joy to be with their granddaddies' old friend's descendants. I was even more thrilled than they were, though. I screamed out (I was drunk on that good beer):

"We're rich!" And I shouted even louder, "Ma! That means you don't have to be a hooker ever again!"

Such embarrassed silence I caused. It was as though the room filled with another load of steam from the kitchen. My biggest faux pas yet. But that dark little Mr. Chiaghazzi stood up, raised his tankard, and yelled, "Here's to hoors, best kind of women I ever knowed!"

I think Mr. Chiaghazzi's toast would have gotten everybody back to their old selves except that Mr. Gambi said, "I think this is all hoopla. Those boys weren't Jean Laffite's sons. Those two boys spread that stuff around themselves. Jean Laffite was too old to have sons by the time he disappeared."

Now this was a horse of a different color.

"Hell, it's true that he was mighty damn old," said Mr. Beluche. "He was sixty-some-odd. But he went ahead and sired two boys all the same. My daddy told me. Hell, nobody's too old! I got some lead left in my damn pencil, I'll tell you all!"

They all drank to that. Then Mr. You said, "My granddaddy was Jean's closest friend from the time they were young men, and he told me that Mr. Laffite's woman was a real lady! No offense, ma'am," he said to my mother. "His woman was even the daughter of a diplomat, and the birth of that second boy killed her and killed Jean Laffite, too. That's how the wondrous Jean Laffite died, of a broken heart. And it was fittin'. He became a scalawag in the first place when the Spaniolis killed his first wife—a little American girl—when he was still a young man. She was sixteen. It was Laffite's loyal servants raised those boys born to the second wife. Raised 'em right here in New Orleans till they came of age."

Then one of the Viking types—by now I was mixing up Mr. Jellness and Mr. Jorness—said to Rexhault, "I remember your mother."

Well, this led to another silence. The blond man cleared his throat and said, "That foreign wench, she was the most famous prostitute on the Mississippi till Laffite's son went on a gambling trip one day disguised as a French nobleman and kidnapped her! Hell, she loved him for doing that to her. They got married and settled right here in New Orleans later, but when he had to disappear, she went back to the Allemagny—or maybe it was Belgique—with a baby is what I heard."

"Heard that myself," said the other Viking.

Then Mr. Beluche said to me, "Little lady, here's somethin' else you should know about your great-granddaddy. My daddy told me that Jean Laffite and his brother, Pierre, were actual French noblemen. Their parents were executed by the peasants during the Reign of Terror. Guillotined because they were of high birth during the Revolution, right along with King Louis and the queen of France. You got a birthright you don't even know about out there in France." He gestured grandly in the direction of the door.

Rexhault stood up, "Before Lily talks me into going off to France, I believed she will need a night's rest." Rexhault turned up his lips in a benevolent smile of dismissal. "I would like to thank you gentlemen for a wonderful evening. As much as I despair at parting from such a fine company, we must be leaving, as we sail tomorrow morning."

News to me. Rexhault pushed up his white cuff and glanced at his Patek Philippe. Mr. Beluche glanced, too.

"Fine wristwatch."

"Thank you."

"How many French francs would you pay for a timepiece like that?"

Rexhault smiled. "It's stainless steel. Five thousand francs."

They all said, "Whoo-ee." Mr. Gambi said, "For that kind of moola, you could hire a boy to follow you around all day for the rest of your life. Want to know the time of day, just give a signal and he'll tell you. Fact is, I would take such a job myself."

We all had a big hoot over that one. Then I asked Rexhault, ''Where are we sailing to, Rexhault?'' hoping to catch him, which I did.

He gave me, my mother, and everybody else a big smile. ''Why . . . to Loggerhead Key. I own it. It was a present from my mother. My mother, the riverboat dolly!''

Chapter 14

My mother bought me sailing whites like hers. Rexhault took us to his beautiful, just-fitted yacht on the Mississippi River. Charles, I found out, also knew about driving boats as well as cars. I thought, Someday, I'm going to get that Charles to smile. The yacht floated gently beside the dock, gleaming in the sun. Many people were around just looking at it and waiting to see who was going to board. And when we did board, members of the press recognized me, because that's their job, especially Picayune photographers. So people began shouting lovely things to me about how proud I'd made them. That kind of chatter still made me want to look around to see whom they were really talking about.

Of course, they were also shouting, "Let's see the medals, Lil!" But the medals were packed away somewhere. I signed a lot of autographs, all the while wondering what I was going to do once I got to Loggerhead Key. I was beginning to feel kidnapped myself. But all I knew was that someday I would meet up again with Gresham Young. That was because, more and more, beginning in New Orleans, I began to think of Miami Beach and Johnny Q and Eddie G as a dream that happened in a faraway night, not a real thing. And I kept fighting at myself to keep it a real thing the way Gresham Young was real, but it wasn't working.

Once my mother and I and Rexhault were all aboard, we leaned on the polished railing and watched trunkloads of our stuff being brought up the gangplank. I joked:

"This doesn't count, Rexhault."

He said, "What doesn't count?"

I said, "This."

"Ah, Lily, that is true. It doesn't count. But though it is not the *Normandie*, it is a beautiful ship, no?"

"Yes, it's a beautiful ship."

"But what you will see in a few days—*that* will count."

"What will I see in a few days?"

"The thing that counts."

"At Loggerhead Key?"

He laughed. "Yes." My mother laughed, too, and shook her head. Then she excused herself, keeping on her beauty schedule. I looked up at Rexhault. He was quite a tall man. I liked him. Right then, I even felt like a daughter being teased by her pop. "Rexhault?"

"Yes, Lily?"

"My mother never thinks about what might happen to her. She doesn't think about next week. She thinks about now. Today. What if, next week, you don't like her?"

"Why, Lily! She's my cousin."

"Oh, sure." The New Orleans beer was now out of my system. "There were probably a million German whores here in New Orleans, and who knows how many crazy ladies."

"I'd like to think that the . . . German lady and the one who was crazy were connected, and we were the result."

"Well, I'd like to, too, but I think you're right now avoiding what's worrying me."

He leaned his full weight into the railing. "You know, Lily, I never think about next week, either. That's probably why I like your mother so much. I let the people who handle my money think about next week. I listen to them carefully. They're like . . . hmmm, let me see . . . they're like my coaches! They keep me from doing foolish things. Such as staying in Germany." He gazed out at the city of New Orleans.

"Don't you want to go back to Germany? I mean, it's your home."

"You know, I don't think of Germany as my home. Not

long after I left Berlin as a young man, I found that I liked having the world as my home. I felt untied.''

''I still feel tied to Miami Beach. I don't want to be untied.''

''I know.''

''But about Ma, Rexhault.''

He said to me. ''One of the many reasons I love your mother is her devotion to you. I am full of admiration for her. And you are a very special person to me.'' Now, he actually got tears in his eyes. ''I promise that no matter what, you and your mother will be taken care of by me.''

Then we hugged. And when we did, I realized that the last man I'd ever hugged was Johnny Q. So I got a mean thought. I hoped Rexhault would get sick of my mother and go back on his word. Then my mother and I could go back to Miami Beach, and she could take up with her old clients who weren't such bad fellas, and I could spend my days back at the bath-club pool.

I was being foolish and selfish, I knew. But I was afraid that the letters from Gresham Young, and maybe listening to Rudy Vallee's rendition of ''We Are Poor Little Lambs . . .'' wouldn't be enough. Enough for what? I wish I knew.

Charles pulled up in the car Rexhault had rented while we were in New Orleans, and a man got out and waved a folder at us. Rexhault signaled for him to be allowed up the gangplank.

''Who's that?''

''He's a sort of detective.''

''What's he want?''

''He wants to show us the results of his hunt, I'd say. The other side of that coin which we heard from those pirates' grandsons last night.''

The man was from Tulane University. A historian. Not a scientist, but he surely did remind me of Professor Gallileo. He was jabbering away even before he was on the boat. And when he got aboard, he waved an old piece of paper under our noses, and said what was on it without having to read it. The paper said: "I leave all my worldly possessions including the lands wrought from my parents in Bayonne, France, to the woman Chou-Chou."

"This will, Excellency, was all my students had to go on. They scattered themselves throughout the city, into the private libraries, through the old houses, into the cemeteries. They fought their way through swamps and Spanish moss and dank water to find this Chou-Chou."

(The Tulane professor was an excellent orator. He and Dr. Gallileo, I just knew, would absolutely make great chums.)

"Of course, Your Excellency, Jean Laffite was an enigmatic and secretive man, which made our task all the more difficult. But his life was recorded whether he liked it or not because of the infamous facts of his history, which, naturally, included his being the first person in America to be granted a presidential pardon for his crimes. Though he was a pirate and a slave trader to boot, his knowledge of New Orleans prevented the British from driving directly up the Mississippi and proclaiming the midsection of our wonderful country for their greedy monarch.

"But pardon or not, hero or not, since he went right back to his former ways, the governor of our wondrous state had no choice but to drive Laffite out!"

I whispered to Rexhault, "Now where have we heard this before?"

"But General Jackson saw to it that Laffite had an acceptable place of exile available to him. A refuge. It was a place that Laffite could keep secret, a place no one cared to even visit, a place that supposedly had no fresh water. History has concluded that he just used this mysterious rock as a stepping-stone while he crisscrossed the Gulf, pillaging and plundering! But he was out of America's hair and knew enough to keep his business in the Caribbean, where he was a constant threat to the islands, to Mexico, and to South America.

"And now, rumor has it that the woman, Chou-Chou, had a child by Laffite's son, and that there is a great deal of activity at Laffite's secret and last home, probably at the direction of just such a descendant!''

He stopped. Rexhault and I were completely entranced. We didn't notice that my mother had rejoined us until we heard her say, ''And did you discover who this Chou-Chou was?''

The Tulane man held his papers to his heart. ''Ah, Chou-Chou . . . my students have fallen in love with her from the rumors and gossip they have uncovered. A great beauty who chose to go off with a debonair gambler knowing full well the day would come when he would desert her. But did he leave her high and dry? No, no, no. He was the son of pirate, and honored a backward code of honor. He gave her everything and went off to start his life again, who knows where. And she sailed back to Europe with the grandson of Jean Laffite.''

''And, sir, did you find out her name?''

We waited expectantly, but the professor's face sobered. He said, ''I regret, madame, that we did not. I'm afraid the woman will remain nameless for all time.'' He smiled. ''Except, of course, for the entrancing moniker Chou-Chou.''

I said to Rexhault, ''So Rexhault, did anyone ever call your mother Chou-Chou?''

He ignored me. Very quietly, Rexhault asked the professor, ''And the name of the waterless key. Was it Loggerhead?''

''But yes, that is the place. I see, Excellency, that you are a step ahead of me here. Loggerhead Key. With the most charming inlet of the whitest sand that squeaks beneath your feet, and backed by a ring of Royal coconut palms that someone—and we'd have to say Jean Laffite—stole from a ship to plant on his key, seeing as how the palms are not native to either of the Americas.''

Rexhault said, ''And this woman Chou-Chou—was there a record of where her home was in Europe? Where she went with the Laffite grandchild?''

''I am sorry, no. I would guess she didn't want anyone to know where she was going.''

* * *

Now this was all great fun, but there was one thing I couldn't help thinking about that no one else was especially concerned over. I didn't expect that Loggerhead Key would sport a thriving university.

Chapter 15

We sailed away from New Orleans, down the bayous, through the swamps, and past the haunts of the pirate who just maybe was my great-grandfather. We took a pirate route through Barataria Bay, a level, limitless mass of soupy water filled with cypress swamps and little islands made of white shells, hanging all over with Spanish moss. It was hard to tell what was water, what was marsh, and what was land. Rexhault's yacht was like an ice breaker, except that the floes and bergs were floating bogs. Descendants of pirates still lived on the islands, and we could see their shrimp boats and pirogues sliding in and out of shrouds of mist that rose from the water like steam.

After the Bay, the Gulf seemed open and clean and free. The kind of water you just want to do a reverse one-and-a-half right into. I hadn't been submerged since New Haven, and my skin was aching. The ache wasn't too hard to take, though, because Rexhault promised me we would arrive at Loggerhead Key by late afternoon.

When we saw leaping marlin in the Gulf, I surely felt as if I were watching a movie picture. It was a beautiful thing, though marlin do create one terrific splash when they crash back into the water. I think that they crashed for fun, and that if they wanted to go in like an arrow they could.

Rexhault signaled one of the fishing boats we would see in the distance, and it approached. Rexhault told us with a twinkle in his eye that the boat belonged to a friend of his he'd spent time with in Madrid.

"I knew he was in the area—he's spending all year here fishing—so I let him know our route to Tortuga today. And here he comes."

My mother, who loves nice surprises, said, "Now tell us who it is, so I can prepare myself."

"When he's not fishing—or carousing. I might add—he's a writer. A great writer."

I was disappointed. "From what newspaper?"

"Well, though he's certainly done newspaper writing, he hasn't been a correspondent for some time."

"Enough, Rexhault," said my mother. "Who?"

"Ernest Hemingway."

My mother was off like a shot. To change. I hung further over the rail and squinted my eyes at the approaching boat.

The boat pulled alongside, and Mr. Hemingway climbed up onto Rexhault's yacht, and when I was introduced to him, he felt my arm muscles. He said, "Lily, you'd haul in a marlin faster than many a man I've fished with." That, my mother told me after he'd had lunch with us and left, was an invitation. To what? I asked. She and Rexhault looked at each other, and my mother said, "To fish."

I told Mr. Hemingway I intended to read all the books I could out on Loggerhead Key, now that I finally have the time, and that I would start with his as soon as I asked my friends on the Yale diving team to send them. He said, "Well, I'm very flattered, Miss Lily. I hope you will let me know what you think of them. And I would be pleased to send you a new book I've written. One that will make some people sorry."

"Sorry for what?"

"Sorry for calling me a cooked goose."

"Oh. Well, I would be happy to read your cooked-goose book, Mr. Hemingway."

He laughed. "Call me, Papa, Miss Lily."

I couldn't.

Rexhault and Mr. Hemingway talked about the war. Mr. Hemingway was very polite to my mother, though she was quite wary of him. She didn't trust him, I could tell. And my mother knew exactly whom to trust and whom not to trust.

In the afternoon, after Mr. Hemingway went along his way, my mother and I stayed on the deck and let the sun burn us. That was the one part of Miami Beach she missed— that breezy, aqua-colored life that kept you cool under the hot Florida sun. The water in the Gulf of Mexico is very clear. My mother and I stared at the water all afternoon, and the sky and the water and the sky again.

Then we made out a string of little dots, the islands of the Dry Tortugas. One island, the farthest to port, was where Rexhault aimed his beautiful yacht. We came closer and closer to Loggerhead Key, and it looked pretty and soft with those hijacked Royal palms all swaying toward Cuba. Rexhault skirted the island just a hundred yards from shore, on around a long spit of rock. The spit protected the spot where so many missing men hid out. The cove was a perfect sandy crescent backed by the magnificent palms, which actually looked out of place on a tiny tropical island because they were so huge and top-heavy, and symmetrically planted.

And sitting smack in the middle of the crescent was the *Normandie*, nestled in the gleaming white sand. Well, not quite the *Normandie*, but close enough to be a promise kept. Rexhault had gone and built a replica of the French liner; seven decks, clipper-ship lines, and porthole windows. Hung above its roof was the real *Normandie*'s electric sign, and it was lit up for us though it was broad daylight. Rexhault said:

"Captain Pugnet saw to it that we got our sign, Lily."

"Oh, Rexhault," I said, "you did it. You really did. It's wonderful."

"I'm glad you're pleased."

My mother was grinning from ear to ear. This was as much her gift to me as it was Rexhault's. She'd put in a lot of hours of hunting to find him. I said, "Ma?"

"Yes, poopsie?"

"Can we swim today? In the Gulf?"

She and Rexhault laughed. They were holding hands. She said, "Why not?"

I swam that day, but not in the ocean. In the pool. And I dived and dived until my mother made me stop to eat. Rexhault's *Normandie* had a terrazzo courtyard in the center of the building, and in the middle of the court was a forty-meter swimming pool with a springboard and a platform.

The entire first floor was open to the sea and filled with breezes, the seven floors of Rexhault's *Normandie* supported by great pillars. These pillars had tropical plants trained around them so they were invisible. There were crystal-block partitions just like in the grand salon of the ship, and they held the light. But the area around the pool Rexhault had not copied from the *Normandie*. He'd copied it from El Morocco in New York City. A replica within a replica.

So the Normandie Hotel, as Rexhault's *Normandie* would be called, contained New York's most popular nightspot, with one grand difference. Instead of four walls, there were three, the fourth not there at all, and these walls were covered with raised carvings of horses and dancing nymphs. The bar looked out onto the swimming pool that had lights built into it. The tables and chairs, though painted gold, were lightweight and could be moved around the pool or under the overhang if it rained. Fluted Egyptian columns supported the floors above, and the columns were of mahogany and gold leaf. There was a piano toward one end of the bar, and it had a veneer of mirrored glass. Big propeller fans hung from the ceiling, in case there wasn't a wind blowing, but there always was a mild breeze coming off the water, through the Normandie, and out the other side. The first floor above the courtyard had four small conference rooms on one side of the pool and a ballroom on the opposite side. Rexhault intended to accommodate the big bands.

My mother said, "Now this is the kind of place meant to be filled with people."

Rexhault said, "And it will be, soon enough, my dear.

The minute we're settled. We will have another port, not exactly for missing men, but for men who . . . now what do we say in New York? Ah . . . for men who want to lie low.''

My mother was going to have fun, I could see that. Her brain was churning as she drifted through the open spaces and walked along the perimeter of the bar trailing her fingers along the rail. ''This is going to be one sensational nightclub,'' she told the air. And it *was* a sensation. A sensation that came to be called the Radar Room, because if you wanted to hear something or if you thought you might hear something, or if there was something worth hearing, you'd hear it there. My mother's Radar Room was the place to be seen before the war years, and a place to do some seeing. Mostly, though, to do some listening.

While I dived that first day, I noticed that there were lots of people about wearing white starched uniforms and smiling at me. These were our maids and maintenance men and waiters and the Radar Room's two bartenders. But Rexhault said we would refer to them as our stewards and bursars and deck crew, etc. It was going to be a grand time, I could see. My mother looked as if she would burst with joy. She and I knew all about big hotels, and we both could tell that this one would surely be a hit. Also, the ''deck crew'' and ''stewards'' were from Cuba, so I could take Gresham's advice after all and learn a new lingo—Spanish. I planned to work on that right away.

On the top floor of the Normandie, I had a sitting room, a bedroom, and a big bath that was practically a locker room with lots of hooks to hang my wet suits, plus a big hair dryer, too. Above my bed was a little shelf, and lined up on the shelf were the Putty Man's small sculptures. Every one. And not a chip or crack in any of them. My mother had protected them with the same care she took with her bottles of nail polish. She was trying to save what had been so dear to me, but what had been—to my mother—just part of a long, painful road that brought her, finally, home.

* * *

In a very short time, the missing men began to arrive. Rexhault's hotel had an immediate international clientele of wheeler and dealers. Friends from his Prohibition days. Black marketeers and smugglers. Modern-day Jean Laffites. Sometimes a few would come with wives or lady friends, but usually they were alone. They didn't stay alone, however. Rexhault called someone in New Orleans, and away went Charles on the yacht, to return with a cargo of twelve very beautiful hookers. Thus, my mother took on a new career. She became a madam.

"Not really, Lily."

"Yes, Ma. Really."

"More like a housemother at a girls' school."

"Ha!"

"Let me explain the difference to you before you go getting your dander up. I'm not going to make these girls sleep with anyone they don't want to. But if they want to, fine, and if they want to accept a gift, monetary or otherwise, fine, and whatever the gift is, they keep it all. But they are getting a fine salary, so the decision is theirs. And they are free to leave whenever they like.

"They are our . . . uh . . . hostesses. Yes, hostesses. I like that. I'm just the foreman. The foreman of a work crew. You were right to laugh at me saying I'd be like a schoolmistress. I'd never be a good schoolmistress, that's for sure. I'm a foreman, and the hostesses are my work crew, and the work will be damn fun!"

"What if the men treat them the way they treated you in Bridgeport? These men are a bunch of gangsters, Ma, in case you didn't notice."

"Shhh! They're not gangsters, Lily, they're . . . they're . . ."

"Oh, stop making up words. Even if they don't carry brass knuckles like Lucky Louie in Miami Beach, people like Lucky Louie work for them."

"I wasn't going to make up a word. I'm just trying to explain things to you so that you'll understand, Lily."

"Ma, I'm beginning to think that the reason I could never

understand what you were talking about is because *you* don't know what you're talking about.''

''Yes, I do, too. Lily, these men are leaders of large organizations.''

''Illegal organizations.''

''Well, shoot. Some laws are silly. Some laws are actually a self-righteous fellow's rules. And rules are meant to be broken. At least the ones made by and for people who prefer to keep their heads buried in the sand. If they don't see it, everything's fine and dandy. Like during Prohibition. More drinking went on during Prohibition than before. But the people who wanted Prohibition were happy, because they were able to believe that—with the law—it just disappeared. Fools!''

''Like prostitution—right, Ma?''

''Exactly like prostitution. And because there's a law against prostitution, there's no one to control it, and that's why a lot of people get hurt. Good and hurt.''

''Ma?''

''Yes, Lily?''

''What if one night in the Radar Room one of the men thinks I'm a prostitute?''

''They won't. And the word is hostess.''

''How do you know they won't.''

She shook her head. ''You're so famous, Lily, but you don't know it. Everyone knows you. Everyone knows you're here. But our customers are the kind who respect people's privacy. Besides, my girls will have feathers and rhinestones. They won't have long Indian braids down their backs.''

''I've decided to cut it.'' I decided that second to cut it. Eddie G was fading back further and further away.

''Aw, Lily, really?''

''Yes. I'm going to have it marcelled.''

''I wonder if your friend Gresham would like that.''

''Well, if he doesn't, he can go peel apples.''

She laughed. ''Atta girl, Lil. And guess what? I think I just thought about Gresham right now because this very minute I see a funny little boat flying the American flag.

Our U.S. Postal Service, I do believe. You can dash him a note and send it out with our mailman.''

I jumped up and ran down to the dock to watch the boat chug along in.

The two sailors from the U.S. Postal Service had a real good time for themselves while delivering our mail. They couldn't believe our Normandie. They couldn't believe our newly arrived hostesses all lounging around the pool, either. They also couldn't believe that all the boxes with my name on them could be for the same Lily Neelan who won two Olympic gold medals. My mother and I treated them to coconut-rum drinks, but without the rum, because they said they were on duty. They were very sad to be on duty right then. And my mother didn't invite them back when they were off duty, either. In fact, they reminded my mother that perhaps we'd have to start thinking about hiring some bouncers for our docks.

The boxes were from the Yale divers. Gresham had spoken to Dr. Gallileo about my wish to go to Yale, and Dr. Gallileo asked the divers if they wanted to take on a little project—seeing that I got a Yale education. How Dr. Gallileo got our address was a puzzlement to Rexhault. Not to me, because who cares? They sent me all the books and course outlines that a first-year man at Yale gets. And my mentor would be Dr. Gallileo, who wrote me such a nice letter about how he agreed *totalmentissimo* with the divers that I was just as entitled to a Yale education as anyone else. He said ''anyone else,'' not ''men.'' As I took the books out of the boxes, I began to think that I might never get to Mr. Hemingway's famous novels.

Before the mail boat left, I wrote a quick thank-you note to Dr. Gallileo, and another to the diving team inviting them to be my guests at the Normandie anytime they wanted. And I told about meeting Mr. Hemingway, and about his cooked-goose book that he would be sending me. I looked up from my fast writing to ask Rexhault if that would be all right with him, and he said, ''Of course, of course.'' I explained that we had great facilities and pointed out how much fun it would be for them to come in the dead of winter and dive under the warm sunshine.

I also sent regards to Gresham in my letter.

The mailmen left, and then I asked my mother if she wanted to join me in getting a Yale education, but she said you couldn't teach an old dog new tricks. So I said that I would ask the hostesses. She thought that was hilarious. I said:

"Ma, you told me they could do whatever they chose to do. Well, there surely is very little to choose from around here. I bet they'd love it, Ma. They work from nine at night till closing. They'll have all day to study with me."

"They need their sleep."

But I got my mother to agree with me that I could make the offer to the hostesses, and it was up to them. I asked them while they were lounging about the pool talking in the sun and doing their nails and such. This was the first time I had ever actually joined the hostesses. Up till then, I'd just give them a nice, "Hello, how are you today?" in passing. They, like everyone else who knew who I was, didn't act like normal folk around me. In fact, with the hostesses, I believe they thought I would be offended if they so much as looked at me. They had a bad picture of themselves, even though they were so beautiful. But I tried to act like a little sister with them, making believe I just didn't even know that they spent their nights with fat old men who smoked cigars. Then, when they finally started to talk to me a little, I gave them my Yale proposition. They didn't think the idea was the least bit hilarious. But the problem was, they told me, that they couldn't read very well. A couple said they could read a little bit, but not much. And they also told me that they didn't see much purpose in their learning now. They seemed sad not to be able to go along with my idea. They all got very blue. So to cheer everybody up, I said, "Why don't we just all take a nice swim, instead?"

To them, a swim meant dunking into the pool up to their chests and then getting right back out again. So after they dunked, I said, "Would any of you like to learn to dive?" Well, a couple of them said yes, but they'd have to get real short haircuts, which was all the rage anyway, so they didn't mind that. I told them diving really kept your body sleek, so then they *all* said they'd like to learn to dive.

The hostesses weren't much better at diving than they were at reading, but they had a good time standing by the edge of the pool, imitating my form. I could see this would be a tough team to coach. Anyway, all their posing attracted Rexhault's guests, and soon the men were all lined up at the railings overhead outside their rooms. The hostesses ignored them. Said they were off duty and told me to never mind the fat men.

Chapter 16

The Radar Room became a well-known place in the world—a necessary monthly visit of the wide network of black marketeers thriving on the war in Europe. And once word got out about what great fun it was, celebrities began to arrive. Soon the Normandie was full of the famous as well as the infamous, where everybody wanted to see and be seen, or, as Henry Fielding put it better, ". . . to do, or to be undone." *Tom Jones* was my favorite book of English literature from Dr. Gallileo. Dr. Gallileo said that it wasn't any wonder to him.

He also told me to take time from my English literature and read Mr. Hemingway's books, which were in transit. He told me I was fortunate to be able to start with *To Have and Have Not* (the cooked-goose book) and work backward. Such a viewpoint would allow for a refreshing commentary on Mr. Hemingway's work.

Whoa, boy, I had my work cut out for me.

A year went by very quickly, busy days and hectic nights all strung together with periodic letters from Gresham Young. It took a year's worth of letters for Gresham to tell me all about himself, bit by bit. Gresham Young was also a missing man.

He told me how, at the end of World War I, his mother had been a displaced person with tuberculosis and a baby. She'd been displaced from England. Gresham's father, an English soldier who was not married to his mother, was killed in Belgium. I imagined Gresham's father to be one of the soldiers talking from under the poppies, like in John McCrae's poem. Gresham told me that Belgium never goes to war, but all the countries around it use Belgium as their battlefield.

Gresham's mother was ostracized by her family because she was unmarried and pregnant and wouldn't tell who her baby's father was, so she took a ship to the United States, where it was discovered she had tuberculosis, something she already knew. She had to go to a sanatorium to live, and rich people took Gresham. Gresham's mother had heard that that was exactly what might happen, so she chanced it, hoping that she could die peacefully, for she was surely dying.

The rich people were the Youngs, and they lived in Cornwall, Connecticut, where they owned a very large dairy farm, and where Mr. Young was a Connecticut legislator as his hobby. Gresham bragged that his stepfather was in the Connecticut legislature longer than anyone else.

The Youngs were in their fifties when they adopted Gresham, and had grown children who were scattered about the world in important international jobs. Mrs. Young had been doing volunteer work with the DP's, and was the one who had to convince Gresham's mother to come out from under a porch outside the immigration building. Gresham's mother was doing two things—coughing up blood and clinging to her baby for dear life. Mrs. Young assured Gresham's mother that she herself would take the baby, and would take good care of the child, as she was an experienced mother. And she promised Gresham's mother that she would bring the baby to the sanatorium every single week for a visit, or more often, depending on the transportation.

Gresham's mother's doctor told Mrs. Young that the ''young lady'' by all reasoning should have been dead months ago, but her will to see her baby safe kept her alive. Before she died, in two weeks' time, all she was able to tell Mrs. Young was that her baby was called Gresham, as that was the family name of her soldier left to die on the Belgium battlefield. Gresham found out through ship's records that his mother's name was Samuela Bishop, and that he surely wasn't interested in finding out anything about her father, Samuel Bishop, who probably lived somewhere in England, hopefully in misery, after disowning his daughter and grandson.

I wondered if one day Gresham would give in, the way Rexhault had, and find out exactly. I was beginning to realize that men lack courage about certain things.

Gresham also wrote that during the years he was a student at Yale, Mr. and Mrs. Young both died. He knew they would die at that time, since they were so on in years. He knew that his new home would be Yale. Even though the Youngs' real children encouraged him to make his home at the dairy farm for the rest of his days, he came to feel more at home at Trumbull College at Yale, with his master, Mr. Warren, and his professors, especially Dr. Gallileo, who was also an orphan. But mostly he would be home diving into the water of the Yale pool.

He said though he made the Olympic team, he didn't win a gold medal because he already had what he wanted more than anything. Security, as Miss Anna Freud would say. He said he didn't have the hunger it takes to be the best.

From these letters, I grew to feel very close to Gresham Young, even though he was far away. And with all the war talk going on, I became worried about more boys dying again in Flanders Fields, and I hoped beyond hope one of them wouldn't be Gresham Young, dying the way his father died and in the very same place.

I wrote Gresham long letters back about my continuing life at the Normandie Hotel.

My life was divided into doing three things: Reading and studying my books from Yale until my eyes would get sore, diving, and allowing the hostesses to treat me like that little sister it turned out they had somewhere back home. They cut and marcelled my hair and gave me manicures and pedicures.

I was not too different from them deep down. They were as devoted to their bodies as I'd been—I, so that I'd be the best diver in the world—they, so that they'd be the best hostesses in the world. When they would give each other massages and mud packs and hot waxes to get rid of body hair (which was painful and turned their skin red for hours), I would read to them. Reading aloud was soothing to them, and to me, too. Trouble was, when someone like Jane Eyre would get really down on her luck, the hostesses would either weep for her or shout at her to pull herself up by her bootstraps. There wasn't any way I could convince them that Jane Eyre wasn't a real person.

The hostesses were all missing, just like the rest of us. I learned that the world throws away a lot of people just because fate left them with no family who cared for them, or friend or home or place to go. I wrote an essay about this for Dr. Gallileo. He gave me an "A" on it and he said that this was the great drawback of capitalism. If you weren't worth money, had no means of making it, had no family to shore you up, you die or you do what my mother did. But only the very strong at heart can will themselves to survive at the expense of their dignity.

In the case of my mother, and as for the hostesses, too, all they had were their attractive faces and fashionable bodies. There were some, like Edith Piaf, who had a voice that picked her up out of Parisian gutters, said Dr. Gallileo, and others like Josephine Baker, who had a personality that lit up the world. So I began to look at our hostesses with more sympathy than I had already.

They had long legs and pouty mouths. They were soft and feminine, but physically very strong as if they'd done hard farm labor all their lives, which was probably the case, my mother said. Every single one of them was saving money to go back to some little town on the mainland where no one would know who they were or what they'd done and meet some nice, established fellow whom they would marry and raise children. That's what looks best to you of anything when, as a child, you've been abandoned.

As time drifted along on Loggerhead Key, there was one thing in the back of my mind that kept pinching me when I'd push it too far back. And when I turned eighteen, it pinched all the harder. That was Miami Beach. And my mother knew that Miami Beach had become something I was dwelling on more and more. She could see it, so she told me that I didn't have to feel obligated to do what I had been so sure I would do when I turned eighteen. She said that since I was happy, why not wait? She said there was nothing wrong with letting the needle on my record get stuck in the groove.

"It's all right to break a promise to yourself, Lily. Let your record go round and round and enjoy this time of your life. Your mind is growing, and I like the way it's growing. Give it a few years, just like those college boys do. Then go out with all that strength and confidence you keep building up and do whatever you want."

"But, Ma?"

"What, honey?"

"I feel like I upped and deserted Johnny Q and Eddie G."

"No, Lily, you didn't. You just spent ten years with them. Ten years to you is more than half a lifetime. To them, it wasn't so long. They knew you'd have to go. They were prepared. I made a big mistake not preparing you, I know. But now things have worked out real well, haven't they?"

"Yes, Ma. But how have things worked out for them?"

"When you're ready to find out, you'll find out."

"What if I don't find them?"

"Well, I don't know about that—if you are determined to find them, you will, heaven knows—but at least you'll have the maturity you'll need if you don't."

So I pushed Miami Beach back to the far side of my brain once more.

Mr. Henderson of *The New York Times* came to our Normandie to do a story. He nearly dropped dead when he saw me. He couldn't believe I was there—the best-kept secret he could imagine, he said. He was worried about me, though. He offered me a place in his home if I ever started thinking about leading a normal life.

I didn't ask him how my oak tree was doing. I was afraid he'd thought the whole thing was a joke. But after he left, he mailed me a picture of the oak tree growing in his back-yard in the Bronx, with his children sitting by it on the lovely lawn.

By the end of 1940, the Radar Room was very full of foreigners. Exiles and deposed royalty and revolutionaries. Within this group were spies. I knew because I was in the Radar Room every day, not for just a week at a time, so I was able to make the connections—who was talking about whom, who was plotting against whom, and who were friends and who were enemies. Not only had I learned Spanish, I was also picking up more and more French and German. I had become a spy myself. I spied on spies. But I thought of it more as eavesdropping. I saw my eavesdropping as part of my studies. Once, I wrote a long paper about Rexhault's guests, only I made up new names for them. I figured my mother would look upon my interest in the guests' intrigues as something political, so it was an activity I didn't much talk about. Instead, I put all the results of my curiosity down on paper and sent it to Dr. Gallileo. Two days after I sent it, my mother said, ''Guess who's coming for a visit? Rum Keg's stepfather.'' My mother referred to Dr. Gallileo as either Rum Keg's stepfather, or ''that crazy Italian.'' I was thrilled to death.

It was very wonderful to see him. He got those Italian opera tears when he saw Rum Keg flying about the Royal palms, free. Rum Keg flew right on down to him and stayed on his shoulder constantly the first day he was here. I told him, See, Rum Keg wasn't dying. He just wanted to have a home. Dr. Gallileo loved the Normandie. Of course, he should have, being a missing man. And he was a missing man, all right—not just because he was an orphan, either.

One night, Dr. Gallileo and I took a walk along the beach. Rum Keg hopped back and forth from his shoulder to mine. The sound of the band playing in the ballroom was muted. Dr. Gallileo talked about how beautiful Loggerhead Key was. He talked about its serenity in a world gone mad. And I couldn't help but notice that his Italian accent was a lot less dramatic than usual. His voice was calm and steady, and there were no arias of tears. When he stopped talking, I asked him how Gresham Young was. He said Gresham Young would love to come and see me more than anything else in the world.

"Then why doesn't he?"

"He doesn't know what to do about you."

"Tell him he doesn't have to do anything. Tell him I really meant my invitation. He can come at a slow time at Yale with his divers, and they can practice—especially the fellows he's got who've made the Olympic team."

Dr. Gallileo stopped and turned to me. Right then, when he looked into my eyes and I looked back into his, I realized he wasn't a crazy Italian at all. His face was different. He said, "Lily, I must tell you something."

I said, "Shoot, Professor."

He said, "This is very serious."

I said, "I can tell."

So he stood there on the beach, in the shadows of the big palms, and gave me a semester's worth of a new subject for me: fascism. He surely hated fascism, and even more, he hated that terrible fellow Mr. Mussolini. He said *ghetto* was an Italian word, an Italian invention. I didn't know what he meant, though. He said, "There are many of us at Yale who act as a conduit to certain agencies in the government. We have great brains at Yale. We are good at analyzing information. At finding the needles in the haystacks."

I said, "You're a spy?" It was hard to put the word *spy* together with Dr. Gallileo.

He smiled. "No, Lily."

That was a relief. Dr. Gallileo wasn't exactly a normal person's idea of a spy—not the male counterpart to Mata Hari, for sure. He could see what I was thinking. He told me what made a good spy. He told me spies needed to be a puzzlement—people you couldn't quite put your finger on. That they must be curious and be thinkers, too. That they must be thought of as perhaps a bit incompetent. That they must not have close ties with family or friends. And that they must have infallible judgment. Mostly, they needed to have a special knowledge of something important, or access to information as a part of their daily, normal life. He said:

"And there has to be a war. The United States is not at war. Not yet, anyway."

We walked back to the hotel. He promised me he'd try to get Gresham to come to visit. He said Gresham was working very hard and needed a rest.

And he did. But the reason was not so much to see me as to cheer up the three divers who wouldn't be going to the Olympics after all. Right after the trials had finished, when everyone was preparing for the Japanese games, Japan declared war on China, and the games were canceled.

They came and we dived. Gresham and I and the diving team were like a bunch of porpoises. We all had grand fun. It was at night when things began to go wrong. I was all dolled up by the hostesses, and Gresham came into the Radar Room and looked at me very strangely, and then he said he was tired and would turn in early. He gazed around. He hated the Radar Room. I felt very bad. One of the divers said, "This is just a little too decadent for Coach."

I'd been very stupid. Here was Gresham probably thinking about the war raging right on Flanders Fields, and thinking of his father, and I thought he'd like to spend the night dancing away. I'd wanted to show off. The hostesses had taught me to dance, and I admit I had a swell time dancing with the divers to get my mind off Gresham's unhappiness. But then I thought, Oh, shoot Lily, just go on up to his room and tell him you're the same old Lily and that you are even intending to grow your braid back.

So I left the room and went up to the floor he was on and was about to knock on his door. The transom was open. I heard low voices. I heard Gresham's voice and the voice of one of our hostesses. Moans, really, not voices. I had to grab both my hands together and squeeze myself tight, or I think I would have thrown up. I ran back to my rooms.

Chapter 17

The next day, Gresham joined me at breakfast by the pool. I was acting aloof and serious and trying not to fidget. He told me that he was very angry with Professor Gallileo. That the professor was using me, and that the letters I wrote to him about the Radar Room could put me in some danger.

I said, "They're just essays, Gresham. Part of my required courses to get my Yale degree." I smiled, he didn't.

He told me that I was being quite cavalier about something that was terribly serious and that I didn't know the meaning of serious and that it was about time I did.

I said, "Dr. Gallileo isn't forcing me to do anything I don't want to do. I have chosen to do this myself. Perhaps it is dangerous. It doesn't matter. I will take the risk."

"Lily, you don't know what you're talking about. And why are you speaking in that strange voice?"

I cleared my throat. I said, "What strange voice?"

"This is not a game."

"Isn't it, Gresham? Isn't it all a game?"

He looked at me as if I had just turned into a mushroom. He said, "Lily, really."

Suddenly, I was very angry. All at once. I stood up. I said, "You know, you make me sick. Who do you think you are, telling me what I should and shouldn't do?"

"My God, sit down."

Everyone was looking at me. I sat down. Now, he tried to apologize to me. He wasn't a very good apologizer. I calmed down, though, and a couple of concerned divers appeared at the table and I saw to it—and it wasn't too hard—that Gresham and I weren't alone together again.

Having your heart broken is no fun, but I hated to see him leave, all the same.

Gresham and I still wrote letters, but they were different from before. We wrote about things other than the Olympics and diving. He apologized for not understanding what my feeling must have been when he was at our Normandie. I tried to explain that, to me, my mother and Rexhault's world was just something to have a taste of once in a while—a break from being a Yale student. He explained that he was very upset with Dr. Gallileo and took his anger out on me. He also apologized for being an old stick-in-the-mud, and said that he quite liked dancing.

I thought, Believe me, Gresham Young, I could tell you weren't an old stick-in-the-mud or I'd have found you in your room alone, not with one of the hostesses, making whoopee. So I made a big decision in my life, and Gresham could tell from the tone of my letters, which reflected my fear and excitement at making such a decision. He kept asking me if I was all right. What I'd decided was to see just what it was that everyone was so cuckoo over when it came to sex. I spent weeks formulating a plan for having sex with one of Rexhault's guests. Or more than one guest, depending on how things went. I didn't want to make any snap judgments.

Fortunately, my decision was helped along by the arrival of a man who looked a lot like Gresham, only fifteen years older. He was a little shy, which appealed to me, considering my growing apprehension. He had no wedding ring. That was important. I was still a moral person, though curious. I made sure he got drunk. I made sure I got drunk. I finagled him out of the Radar Room while everyone was going crazy over a hypnotist act Rexhault had brought in. We left while a lady weaved in and among the tables doing an imitation of a chicken, which the hypnotist convinced her she was.

We took a drunken walk along the beach. It was a dark night, with no moon and clouds blocking the stars. I sat down under some overhanging hibiscus bushes and started to cry. Crying had not been part of my plan, though it was just what the doctor ordered. This man got very tender trying to comfort me, and the next thing he knew, and I knew, was that he was sticking his . . . well, his weenie in me, and I never opened my eyes till it was over, since I kept trying to imagine that he was Gersham. Having a man's weenie in mine didn't feel too bad. Actually, I kind of felt a little thrill.

I left him lying on the beach, dead asleep under the hibiscus, and hoped he would think he'd dreamed the whole thing. I think I told myself that he'd believe it was a dream so that I would feel less ashamed about using somebody. But the next day, because he was such a decent fellow, he came over to me while I was reading the sermons of Cotton Mather and apologized for his outrageous drunken behavior. He hoped he hadn't taken advantage of me. I told him he hadn't. He was greatly relieved. I felt like dog duty. But at the same time, when I went back to reading, I didn't think that what I had done would qualify me for time in Reverend Mather's hell, where worms would feast on my eyeballs.

So I found that sex was a little thrilling, but that using somebody was something I didn't intend to do again. The next time, I would have to let myself be used, not that I wanted to be a martyr. The next fellow I picked was what you'd call a ''lady's man.'' Watching this man over the past year on his monthly stops at the Radar Room had allowed me to size him up. He was exactly what I was looking for. A conqueror. I'm sure his belt was notched. He always was interested in our most popular hostess. He flirted incessantly with my mother. And when he looked at me, it was like a man looking at what would have to be the greatest challenge of his life. Not that he tried anything. Rexhault would have had him drowned.

He was a Cuban. Cubans were the rage among the hostesses. He was a very handsome Cuban, too. One look from me, and he knew what I was asking for. He walked by me in the Radar Room and whispered to me without moving his lips, "Three o'clock. My boat."

I stepped onto his giant yacht at 3:00 A.M. He made love to me for two hours. The first time took five minutes, about four and a half minutes longer than it took with the first fellow. When he was done with the first time, he apologized for being so fast. I said, "Oh, that's all right." The second time took the next two hours. That's when I found out that there are things a man can do to a woman's body that are pretty embarrassing to think about, but feel like going to heaven. When we were done and the first crack of dawn was showing, I told him in a very nice way that I would never do that with him again, but thank you very much. His face was shocked. I think it was the same for him as it would be for me if Dr. Gallileo gave me an "F" on a paper and I was expecting an "A." The Cuban man didn't get angry or anything, he just couldn't imagine that I wasn't fulfilled, and he never looked me in the eye again when he came to the Radar Room after that.

So my curiosity was satisfied, and I could understand why Gresham chose to spend an evening with a hostess rather than with a bunch of loud people, and I thought that there was a lot of injustice in that he couldn't have spent that night with me. The rules that govern sex are stupid and definitely made to be broken.

The next year, just after Thanksgiving, the Japanese attacked Pearl Harbor, and FDR declared war. All the Yale divers, every Yale man, actually—including Gresham Young—wanted to go and fight. I began to wonder if all the colleges and universities would shut down. They didn't, but Olympic training did. Then I wondered if there would ever be any more Olympic Games.

And just as Captain Pugnet had forewarned, the *Normandie*—the real one—would have to go to war, too. The *Normandie* happened to be in New York Harbor when FDR declared war, so the ship was immediately seized by the U.S. Navy. In wartime, a lot of rules are thrown to the winds, and privateering comes back in vogue. The work on the French liner would begin immediately, and she would be refitted as a troop ship to transport soldiers back and forth from Europe. What a shame they couldn't send the soldiers to Europe on her just the way she was. That would have been very nice for the boys. I could just picture the Whiffenpoofs singing in the grand salon for their fellow soldiers.

But, anyway, down came the letters on her clippered bow, and she became officially known as the U.S.S. *Lafayette*. But no one ever called her that. There wasn't enough time to paint her gray and stencil on new white letters. The U.S. Navy wasn't very clever at dismantling ocean liners.

Rexhault sent his regrets to Captain Pugnet—Rexhault was actually quite distraught—and got a message back from Captain Pugnet telling him that everything on the *Normandie* that could be detached from her would either be put in storage or sold. So for the first time in almost four years, I would be going back to the mainland with Rexhault, while my mother held down the Radar Room, which was surely jumping.

Rexhault wanted to purchase some tapestries for our Normandie's ballroom, and also several of the Lalique stanchions for the Radar Room. He had fond memories of the glow they gave off, just as I had. "You and I, Lily," he said, "are like a couple of moths."

And he especially wanted the grand piano—a wonderful Steinway—from the *Normandie*'s smoking lounge, where he and my mother had sat together each night listening to Irving Berlin and Cole Porter and George Gershwin. He thought we needed a nice, quiet, romantic little lounge at the hotel, as people were becoming more and more secretive, it seemed to him.

Rexhault and I would go to New York, where he would spend several days arranging his *Normandie* bids, and I would spend a couple of days in New Haven visiting Dr. Gallileo and the divers and Gresham Young. I decided not to tell them I was coming, so that they wouldn't fuss. I had to tell them good-bye before they went off to fight the Japs or the Jerries. I did think about Miami Beach, but Mi-

ami Beach was behind my thoughts of Gresham, and they
would have to stay there for the time being.

When we got to New York, and before I went in Rexhault's car to New Haven, we both went directly to Pier 42
to look at the great ship. We didn't even have dinner first,
Rexhault was so anxious to get to the *Normandie*. It was a
horrible sight to see. This grand liner, more beautiful than
anything else made by human hands, was being stripped in
front of everyone. It was a very grim thing to happen to her.
There was a line of men like ants carrying out her beautiful
insides. I thought of the word *hysterectomy*, which was an
operation several of our hostesses had to have where they
worked before. As soon as Rexhault saw one of the officials
in charge of the operation, he made plans to go to the warehouse, where everything would be brought. He couldn't
stand it. Then he and I went to our hotel. We ate in our
room, and said good night and not much else. I told him I
would see him in two days, and to try not to feel so bad.
War is hell.

The next morning I rode along the Merritt Parkway
through the bare Connecticut woods worrying about seeing
Gresham. I tried to chat with Rexhault's driver, forgetting
that Charles didn't chat. My mother told me that perhaps
this visit would be a way to get Gresham out of my system.
She told me that an obsession with the first boy who'd every
kissed me was something to be expected, but that such an
obsession when carried along for too long a time was also
unnatural. I thought maybe I'd see just what it was that
made me obsessed with him, and of course I saw exactly
what it was as I watched him from against the wall of the
pool. He hadn't seen me slip in.

He was putting the boys through their paces. I watched
the practice and took in every move Gresham made and
every word he said. He was an exciting coach. It was really
like watching part of myself, and not only part of myself; I
saw everyone in him—everyone I'd loved: Johnny Q and
Eddie G and Mr. Fraley and Rexhault and the Putty Man
and even Mr. Marvin Modeen, whom I hadn't loved. He
was what I was, what I loved about living—his understand-

ing of diving, his empathy with divers, his being a coach and a gentleman and also being a missing man.

So who cares? I thought. If this was an obsession, then some obsessions must be okay to have. After all, I loved diving with such a great intensity that that was surely an obsession, too.

I kept watching Gresham and analyzing. I felt affectionate toward him in the same way I felt toward Rexhault. I looked up to him the way I did to Johnny Q. I felt a great admiration for his talent, the same talent that Eddie G had, and the suffering both he and Eddie G had felt. And mostly, I trusted him. A special kind of bottomless trust, the way I trusted my mother.

When the practice ended, I stepped forward and said, "Hello, Gresham."

Before I was mobbed by his team, I got to see the instant of affection in his eyes that I'd hoped desperately for. When he looked at me, his expression was gladness. He was glad to see me. Hooray! But then all the things that worried him swam into his eyes, and his face clouded. That, I expected, but at least now I knew that it would be impossible for him not to show me some attention, though he had a will of steel. After I shook hands with all his team, he shooed the boys to the showers.

"Hello, Lily."

"Hello, Gresham."

I put out my hand and he looked at it, and then he took it and held it lightly. I thought an electrical crackle noise might sound from where the skin of our palms pressed together. He said, "Dr. Gallileo will be so thrilled to see you."

"I'll be thrilled to see him."

"He says you're about to graduate first in your class."

We both smiled.

"Let me change, Lily, and I'll walk you over to his office."

While we walked in the wind, through the beautiful buildings of Yale, all of it so different and so much more real than our Normandie at Loggerhead Key, I was feeling

very smug, knowing that, eventually, Gresham would have
to face being alone with me. He was a gentleman, and he
wouldn't refuse my dinner invitation. But while we walked,
protected from the discomfort at being together by the buf-
feting wind, we talked, expanding on what we'd told each
other in our letters. We wondered together what would become of the Olympic Games if the war lasted a long time.
Everyone said we'd whip the Japs and the Jerries in a very
short time, but Gresham and I could tell it would take a
long time: I knew because I'd had a Yale education (make-
shift though it may have been), and learned about war, and
Gresham because not only did he have a Yale education, but
he could feel the magnitude of the war in his bones.

We passed the statue of Nathan Hale. There was something in the granite of Nathan Hale's face that was in Gresham's face, too, though I didn't mention that to him.
Gresham was worried about the boys on his team especially.
While he talked about them all signing up and what that
would mean, I thought about Germans using gas again and
the gas spreading around the earth and killing all of us.
Gresham told me that he'd be leaving the next week. He
was going to be part of a new government organization that
had been formed at Yale. I said, "Organization?"

He said, "Yes."

I said, "What kind of organization?"

He said, "It's a combination of several government . . .
services."

"Called?"

"The OSS."

"What's that stand for?"

"Office of Strategic Services."

"So you'll be in this organization instead of going off to
war?"

"Well, I will be leaving the country . . . as part of my
duties with the organization."

"It sounds fearful to me, Gresham. Why are you doing
this?"

"Part of the Yale tradition."

Nathan Hale was a Yale man. "Will I know where you are?"

"I don't know."

"What will you do in the OSS?"

"Dive."

"I thought so."

He laughed. "Only you would have thought so."

I could tell he didn't want to be asked about any of it, but I didn't have to ask. Gresham would probably be jumping into the drink somewhere to set up the next guy in this OSS chain to do God knows what. I intended to ask Dr. Gallileo about that, to see if I was right. Even though I came up with a rational explanation of what Gresham would be doing during this war, it still brought tears to my eyes. But then, here was Dr. Gallileo who could burst into tears in a second, so he and Gresham thought I was crying at the joy of seeing him.

He hugged me and danced me around his office and got his Rube Goldberg coffeepot rolling, and we all drank out of his little cups while I told him about Rum Keg and his adventures in his new home. Mostly how he flew all over the island now, but returned to his perch every night in the open end of the Radar Room. I said how he loved the music and the commotion and that he was only afraid of other birds, and how we recently got him a couple of kittens so he'd have some friends.

Gresham was looking at me strangely. I said, "I never really got to show Gresham the nice things about living in a big hotel on an island. He only saw the decadence."

Gresham didn't say anything. Dr. Gallileo detected a little bit of discomfort, and so he got very serious and thanked me for the work I'd done for him. He said it would help us beat the Fascists and the Nipponese, and I was glad to have Gresham hear how Professor Gallileo had faith in me. In fact, I think the professor put a little bit of a show on because he knew I wanted Gresham to think more of me than he did. Dr. Gallileo is such a pal.

Dr. Gallileo invited us to dinner with him. He said, "We

will go to a place I know that is very festive. Lily, did you
bring a pretty dress?''

I surely had.

I left them together thinking how Gresham liked being
around Dr. Gallileo—trusted him—as I did. We needed
fathers.

I went to the hairdresser at my hotel. My marcel had
grown out a lot, so she was able to pull my hair back tightly
and put the ball of curls into a silver net. I stared at myself
in the mirror. From the front, I looked the way I looked
when I had my braid. I wore a black dress. The skirt was
swishy chiffon. The top of it looked like a plain black bathing suit. But I didn't look like a girl diver. My dress had no
back—just a fine, thin crisscross of rhinestones. I looked
like a woman.

A beautiful Italian restaurant was hidden behind an old
warehouse door. And it was very festive, because people
thought our boys were going to run off and win a war in a
couple of weeks, and that this was something to party about.
In the entry, the *maître d'* slid my fur coat off my shoulders,
and Gresham and Dr. Gallileo gaped at me. I said:

"What's the matter with you two?"

Professor Gallileo said, *"Ah, che bella figlia!"* and went
into minor weeping. Gresham smiled at me and said, "You
look lovely, Lily."

I said, "Well, thanks."

The *maître d'* knew the professor and got him calm right
away so that he could show us to our table and not hold up
the people behind us. The restaurant was packed full, and
I recognized the sound of Tommy Dorsey's band and his
incredible trombone playing. Tommy Dorsey knew how to
lead a band—a band that included an entire string section.
And at the same time, he could play his trombone and see
what was going on all around. While we walked across the
floor, as if by magic, the band just sashayed out of "Be-
witched, Bothered and Bewildered," and right into "South
of the Border, Down Mexico Way," which was as close to
a song about Loggerhead Key as Tommy could get. I waved,
and he waved back. He'd been at the Radar Room the week

before. Our waving made everyone stare at me, and a lot of whispering started up. We were given what was obviously the VIP table, so I hoped no one really important would come in.

Professor Gallileo and Gresham and I ate like three pigs at a trough, the food was so delicious. I told our waiter to please tell the chef that it was the best meal I'd ever had in my life. I was in a very happy mood—Italian food and Tommy Dorsey playing and Gresham looking very handsome in his dinner jacket and Professor Gallileo forgetting about the Fascists for a little while. The chef came out and kissed my hand, and he and the professor had another little weep together. I said to Gresham:

"Don't you love Italians?"

He said, "Some."

Faux pas. But Professor Gallileo said, "Tonight, we will forget about the bad ones. Tonight, we will dance. Right now. And, Gresham, I will dance with Lily first, because I am an old man and cannot stay out half the night. Soon you will have her all to yourself, but for now, she is mine."

And Tommy Dorsey sashayed his band once again, out of "There'll Be Bluebirds Over," and into "Return to Sorrento." The professor was a good dancer but very formal, staring straight over my head as he waltzed me around. I tried to dance as regally as possible, so he would be proud. And then, after the dance, the professor seemed to just lose his spirit, and I cried some Italian tears when he insisted on leaving so that Gresham and I could be young and carefree. We said good-bye. And when he left, Gresham said, "He's very worried. He's Jewish, you know."

"Oh. I didn't know."

The waiter brought us two tiny glasses of an Italian drink that could have been called liquid gold. Gresham and I clinked the two little glasses together, and the drink tasted like liquid fire, not liquid gold, but the aftertaste was something wonderful.

Gresham said, "Couldn't describe the taste of this if I wanted to."

I agreed. Then everyone was applauding because Frankie

Sinatra was walking up to the mike. Gresham and I clapped, too. There was no voice like Frank Sinatra's, just as there was no drink like our Italian gold. Frankie's voice filled the room, and he sang, "I'll Never Smile Again." Gresham asked me to dance.

I fit very easily into Gresham's arms. My cheek brushed his once, and the second time my cheek brushed his, it stayed there. Against his. And I got tears in my eyes just as easily as the professor did, so I whispered, "Gresham?"

"Yes, Lily?" he whispered back.

"Nothing."

He pulled away from me a little and looked into my eyes. I said, "I guess I just felt like saying your name."

He pulled me back closer to him again with his face against mine, and I thought, If only I could stay exactly like this forever. With each passing second, as we danced, I was able to feel the bits and pieces of the feeling of being in Gresham's arms. I felt my breasts pressed against his chest, and that was the same as if I'd just swallowed a quart of honey. I felt my thighs against his, and like the Italian drink, it was an indescribable sensation. And then his hand moved slightly on my back, and I could feel his warm fingertips against the skin of my back and I willed his hand to stay there. It did. We danced for three dances, and then Tommy went into "Chattanooga Choo-Choo," and Gresham and I sat down, and I knew he felt just as I did, because he didn't let go of my hand at the table. One of my knees touched one of his knees.

We were the last to leave the restaurant. Rexhault's car was parked right in front of the door. We got in, and Charles drove off. Gresham put his arm around me and kissed me very softly. But it was up to me. I said:

"Gresham, I would like you to come to the hotel with me. Stay with me."

He said, "I don't know."

And in my panic not to let him slip away from me, I said what was the stupidest thing I could have. Worse than a faux pas. I said, "I'm not a virgin, Gresham." He didn't say anything, and maybe if I'd left it at that, things would have been all right, but then I kept going because he hadn't answered and I never knew how to keep quiet, so I said, "I've had sex with two different fellas after you left the Normandie last year. So you don't have to feel that . . ."

His eyes opened wide. He said, "Lily," in an upset way.

So then I said, "I mean, since you went to bed with one of our hostesses, I thought . . ."

He took his arm from around my shoulders, leaned forward, and said to Charles, "Pull over!"

I said, "What's wrong?"

He said, "Everything. I'll be leaving in two days. I prefer to remember this night up until a few minutes ago."

"Well, I prefer to remember everything. Like when you came to our Normandie and spent hours talking to me and training with me and your boys all day and half the night, and then you going off to bed with a hostess, and my wondering why you were a . . . a . . . stick-in-the-mud. . . ."

"Lily, stop it."

"I mean, at least when I did it, I waited until you weren't around to see me."

"I said, Stop it. You're, you're . . ."

"I'm what?"

"You're not what you seem."

"I'm not? Of course I am. How do I seem?"

"You seem like an angel."

"Well, I'm surely not that. I'm a human being. I'm exactly like you."

"I'm a man."

"Oh! I see! A man is somebody who thinks that there are two kinds of women, hookers and angels. Well, we're all both. We're—"

He got out and slammed the door. I shouted, "Charles! Drive. Go."

I was so angry. I felt like my mother when she walked off Harry's porch when he expected her to peel his apple. Except Gresham was the one who got to storm off, not me. So I took off my shoe, rolled down the window, and threw the shoe at Gresham, though of course we were much too far away for him to notice such a thing. But I hoped he heard me shout into the night, ''Damn you!''

Damn him. I went to sleep thinking, Damn him, damn him, damn him! I woke up every five minutes. When I could see the light of day through the curtains, I still went back to sleep again. The maid at one point touched my shoulder to tell me it was noon, but I told her to go away. The phone rang around three. I'd told the desk I wouldn't take any calls. I got angry all over again. The phone rang and rang. Then I remembered I told the desk I wouldn't take any calls unless it was an emergency. I sat up and picked up the receiver. It was a man crying. It was Rexhault. I thought my mother must have died. I couldn't hear what he was babbling. Then I could. He said:

''The ship is on fire. A terrible fire. The *Normandie* is burning. It is being destroyed. It's too horrible.''

I realized why I was having such a bad time understanding him. The sounds of fire engines and sirens were all but drowning him out. I said, ''Are you at the pier, Rexhault?''

''Yes. Oh, God, Lily, half an hour ago I could see the smoke from my hotel window. I knew it was the *Normandie*. I didn't know why, but I knew.''

''I'm coming right now, Rexhault. As fast as Charles can drive.''

''No, no, don't come. I just had to speak with you. To someone who . . .''

''I'm coming, Rexhault.''

''Lily, that beautiful ship . . .''

''I'm coming.''

I hung up. A fire. My turn for a fire. And I kept seeing flames and parrots and my granny and burning cats. Then, while I was washing, I imagined the shining satin bedspread on my stateroom bed on the first-class deck of the *Normandie* burning up. It was deep dark purple, and very puffy. And then I thought of Pearl Harbor, and the *Arizona* burning with all the sailors in their beds without any purple bedspreads. Then I thought of Gresham. I called him at the pool. I didn't know how upset I was until I heard my voice on the phone, quaking, as I asked for him. And when I heard his voice, I told him I loved him and that there was a war and he was going to it and that I didn't want him to be gassed and that the *Normandie* was on fire and I had to go to New York and help Rexhault. I felt scared and alone. I knew I'd be no good with Rexhault, who needed my mother, not me. Gresham said:

"I'll be at the hotel in ten minutes. Don't go anywhere."

So I waited, and then he was there and he told me he'd never dreamed he could love anyone so much as he loved me and I apologized over and over and I held on to him and he held on to me.

We got in the car. Charles drove very fast to New York. Charles handed me a small bag. I opened it, and my shoe was inside. I thanked Charles, and in the mirror his facial expression never changed, even though it couldn't have been too much fun for him to go out at 5:00 A.M. looking for a shoe. I explained to Gresham about how I'd thrown my shoe at him. Gresham's facial expression surely changed. He smiled and so did I, and we even laughed a little bit, when I was sure I'd never laugh again in my life. I snuggled against Gresham's chest and thanked God for whatever He might have had to do with it.

Right when we crossed from Greenwich into New York we could see the smoke, and Greenwich is a forty-five minute drive from Pier 42. It was black smoke. Poor Rexhault. I knew he was someone who needed comfort nearby twenty-four hours a day, and my mother was a thousand miles away. I asked Charles if he could speed it up.

Chapter 18

The area around the pier was pandemonium—hundreds of people milling about, and fire apparatus snaking over every surface. Above the chaos rose the *Normandie*, high and mighty as ever, but with smoke pouring out of her. And she was listing. Just a bit. Some people were arguing that she wasn't. But I was trained to know straight and tall and level and balance. That ship was leaning. Gresham said it was, too, unmistakably.

Rexhault had people looking for us. A couple of policemen led Gresham and me to Rexhault, while Charles, guarding the car, kept track of our movement through the crowd. Rexhault was holding court with several official-looking men. He was not as his voice would have had me think. I could see that now he was mostly angry. He took a moment from his discussion with the men and hugged us both. I said:

"She's listing, Rexhault."

He said, "I know. The fireboats have filled her with water. There are three thousand men on the ship—firemen, police, dock workers, sailors—and none of them know what they are doing."

The group he'd been huddled with came over to us, escorting a fellow in a uniform with a lot of gold decorations on it. One of the men said:

"Here is the admiral, Rexhault."

Rexhault said to the admiral, "The seacocks must be

opened. She must be balanced immediately. If she is balanced, she will sink into the river bottom just below her. It is soft mud, and it will keep her upright until—''

The admiral interrupted, ''May I ask, sir, if you are a German national?''

Rexhault pulled himself up to all his tall Excellency. ''I am an American citizen.''

''Good. And I am an admiral in the United States Navy. The navy will handle this, thank you very much!''

The admiral turned on his heel and was gone. Rexhault's group of men looked at each other, and then in one motion looked to the ship. Their eyes said so clearly that the *Normandie* was lost. The U.S. Navy wouldn't be able to do it, not with that damned fool of an admiral. The quiet in our group seemed to spread. Now, there was no mistake. The ship's list was undeniable. It was as if the curtain had risen on a play; the crowd went from loud talking to mumbling to a hush.

As if on cue, the silence was broken by a series of small explosions, like cherry bombs going off on the Fourth of July. One of Rexhault's men said calmly that the noise was the lamps bursting from the heat. Rexhault put his arm around me. Nobody would ever see Mr. Lalique's crystal stanchions again. Poor Gresham. He wanted to do something when he saw how the noise pained me, but there was nothing for anyone to do. Then there came a terrible crack, and I was sure it was a big tree hit by lightning. But there were no trees and no lightning. It was one of the dozens of ropes—each as thick as a seaman's waist—that secured the *Normandie* to the pier. One rope had snapped, and now it flew out like a snake. People began to run for cover as there came another loud crack and another. The great ropes ripped about wildly before falling down into the water. The last rope gave way, and when it did, the ship actually swayed to port away from the pier. The gangplanks plopped down into the water, and the men fighting the fire on the decks were all falling over and tumbling into each other.

A wind came off the water and blew the smoke down onto the pier, and the air was instantly black. Gresham and Rexhault and I grabbed each other. We were blinded, and then we began to cough and choke. Another wind lifted the cloud away, and when it was cleared, I was sure the *Normandie* would be gone, but she had held, tipped over several degrees. Now, attention was turned to getting the scores of men futilely fighting her fires off her.

As dusk fell, reports came that the fire was under control, but we were to learn later that the admiral's chain of command had broken down, so no one had the authority to tell the fireboats to stop pumping water. The U.S. Navy couldn't locate its admiral. He was nowhere to be found, so arcs of seawater from the fireboats continued to fill the *Normandie*, and the ship maintained its listing as slowly and surely as a minute hand on a clock—too slowly to see, but we all were aware that the cargo ports were now at the waterline. They hadn't been just ten minutes earlier.

Great spotlights came on. In the yellow glow, we could see the faded paint where the letters of the ship's name had been spelled out on its bow. The faint, ghostlike name, NORMANDIE, was pitiably appropriate as the ship's spirit tapered out. Rexhault said:

"The French will never understand our letting this happen. Another thing to further demoralize them."

We were shivering with the cold, but we didn't notice. Rexhault and Gresham and I, and everyone else, couldn't leave her.

The worst came just before midnight. The pier was eerily and utterly quiet, and everyone turned as the admiral's big car abruptly appeared, screeching to a halt a few feet from where we stood. He got out, slammed the car door, took one step toward the ship, and turned to stone. It seems he'd been told that the fire was out, not that the ship was listing. He went into action. He ordered all the news photographers out of the area. He told the police to break any cameras that they spotted. Soon he was screaming like a crazy person, while everyone stared at him.

Rexhault said we should leave. We would walk back to our hotel. Charles had been forced to move the car long before. We found out later that he'd been looking for us the whole time. As we crossed the street, I looked over my shoulder one time just as I did the night I was with my mother, the night I saw the *Normandie*'s electric lights go on. Now, in the horrible aura of the spotlights, I watched as the huge ship began to go over, and she paused once, as if making one last, prodigious effort to right herself. Then she turned completely over onto her side, and lay down and died. Rexhault and Gresham pulled me away with them, and we all three wept.

Charles found us several blocks from the pier and drove us to the hotel. I told Rexhault that Gresham would clean up in my suite. I said that we'd see him in the morning, so that we could have a beautiful breakfast together before he had to leave for his war duty. Rexhault agreed, though his face showed no expression when he said good night to us in the lobby of the hotel. We watched him go off to the bar with Charles. In the elevator, I sank into Gresham's arms, and we held each other. No, we supported each other.

When I crossed the threshold of my hotel room with Gresham, I felt just as I felt passing beyond the point of no return thousands upon thousands of times at the edge of a diving board, my body leaning just barely enough forward so that there was no going back. I believe that the way I could manage to hold that moment was what made me a champion. Gresham's divers had told me that they couldn't believe how long I would remain, poised, in the middle of no-man's-land. Spectators weren't aware of that tiny pause; they just watched and tensed waiting that one extra millisecond before they rose right along with me as I presented my form, became an arrow, and disappeared into the pool, no splash.

Gresham knew all about that millisecond, too. I told him it was a gift, an accident, that I could do that. And he said it was an accident perfected by a lifetime of practice and the best coaches I could have had.

So there I was again, and I felt the millisecond, and this time I lost my balance. I swayed. Gresham took me to him. He said, "We don't have to, Lily."

But I could feel the tremble in his body, and I could feel it in mine. He shut the door behind us with the hand that wasn't holding me.

Gresham put his arms around me and rested his forehead against mine. He said, "I love you, Lily."

I said, "I love you, too."

He kissed me. It was the same kiss he gave me four years ago when I was sixteen. That same kiss that was meant to be brotherly, but because I had no brothers and he had no sisters, we didn't know that the dry brush of our lips would make us so irresistible to one another for such a long time afterward.

Then he kissed me again, and this kiss was slow and soft and I felt as if I were sinking into it, and I sensed an involuntary yielding to what had once been so fearful. Though I was sure I'd be apprehensive about making love to Gresham if the time should ever come, I wasn't. I looked directly into his face. I said:

"I feel very dirty."

He said, "Oh, no, Lily."

I smiled. "Gresham. I meant the soot."

I took both Gresham's hands and turned them palms up. They were black, like mine. Everything we'd touched outside had been layered with ash. "I think we need a shower. First."

Chapter 19

We were covered with grime. We could not see the lights of New York City through the tall windows. The windows were blocked by the ash. The windows of the wondrous St. Regis Hotel on Fifth Avenue, where they have fresh flowers on a small gilt shelf in the elevator.

Gresham looked into my eyes. We were both brimming over with anxiety. So I said, "And we should throw our clothes away."

That gave him something to smile about, and I felt him relax. "And then what will I wear after our . . . shower?"

"We'll send for some clothes."

He laughed. He hugged me again. He said, "You make everything simple." I settled into his hug. "Lily, I have to leave you so soon."

"But we'll keep writing. And I'll see you when you have a leave. I'll bet you'll have a leave after they train you for whatever it is you'll be doing."

"I've been trained."

"You have?"

"Lily . . ."

"Never mind. Kiss me again."

He did. The pressure of his hands on my back and the length of his body pressed against mine made me think of when we were dancing at Professor Gallileo's restaurant. I laid my face on his shoulder and he laid his cheek against the side of my head. I opened my eyes. I saw the bed through the doorway. The brocade coverlet had been turned back. The sheets were very white. I sighed, not wanting to stop feeling him against me, but knowing we had to let go of each other.

"What is it, Lily?"

"Gresham, I've lived in a pool all my life. I need to be clean."

He pulled away. "So do I."

The bathroom was ornate, full of gilt and crystal lighting. There was a short, deep bathtub and a shower enclosure. The door to the shower was etched glass. The bathroom was as bright as the *Normandie* before it was destroyed. I pushed that thought away. Gresham and I looked at each other's reflections in the glass. No one could have possibly guessed that I had blond hair. "I hope there's lots of shampoo in here."

"I'm sure there is."

"We'll have a great head-scrubbing."

Everything I said seemed to make him laugh. That made me feel very gratified. He was quite a serious person when I wasn't making him laugh. We took off our coats. "I don't want to ever smell like a burnt ship again," I told him.

I pulled off my shoes. He took off his. He wore soft socks. My toenails had been painted shell pink by a hostess before I'd left Loggerhead Key, and they looked like seashells under my silk stockings. He started to unbutton his shirt. I watched him take it off. His shoulders had the most elegant muscles, sculptured. I could see how hard his muscles were beneath his undershirt.

I was wearing a sweater dress with a tie belt and buttons all the way down the front. Gresham dropped his shirt on the floor and then he untied my belt. Then he unbuttoned the first few buttons of my dress until my dress was open enough that I could just let it slide down my arms and fall off of me. I stepped out of it. Gresham unbuckled his belt buckle and took off his trousers. He stood in front of me in his white undershirt and drawers and socks, and he had curly dark hair on his legs and fine black hair on his arms. It felt very erotic to stand together in our BVD's, which was very curious to me, as we'd both stood together before, many times, nearly naked in wet bathing suits clinging to our bodies like a new coat of paint.

I lifted up my slip to unhook my stockings. I put one foot up on the vanity and rolled my stocking down my leg the way my mother did instead of my usual way of just dragging a stocking off one leg while I hopped around on my other foot. It seemed that doing it my mother's way would be a nice thing for Gresham. He stared as I took each stocking down over my thigh, over my knee, and off my foot. He said, very quietly:

"Oh, my God."

I said, "Oh, your God?"

"I mean, I love you, Lily. I love you."

I took off my garter belt and stood in my camisole top and my teddies that had no lace but at least were light blue, which is a color that looks nice against my skin.

He crossed his arms and pulled his undershirt off in one motion, and his quick, coordinated muscles stirred my soul.

"You're so beautiful, Gresham."

He smiled at me.

I said, "I love the way you take off your shirt."

"How do I take off my shirt?"

I said, "Like this." And I crossed my arms and lifted my camisole over my head and off all in one motion. I dropped it. He stared at my breasts. I felt the presence of my bare breasts. Oranges. Gresham's body seemed to be moving toward me, though he hadn't moved toward me yet.

I slipped my teddies down and said, "C'mon." I stepped away from him through the glass doors into the shower. My back was to him as I turned on the water, and when I turned around again, the water and Gresham, too, completely covered me and were over me and on all sides of me.

In the shower, we kissed and washed and shampooed. The scar under his hair that I felt with my fingertips kept me from fainting, I think. We just got lost in bubbles and warm, clean water, while the world outside stopped existing. Just as I began to feel lost in outer space, Gresham's soapy hand was sliding between my legs and it made me

have an orgasm, and when the orgasm stopped, I felt frantic
with emptiness, because there should have been more. So I
pulled him out of the shower, and we were wrapping each
other in towels, and we somehow got to the bed and lay
down and then he was inside of me and everything was filled
up and I gasped and hugged him and rolled over with him
inside of me and then rolled back and he pushed so hard
that I hung on to him for dear life, knowing how soon he
would be gone away from me. And then we were done.

We rested. He raised my hand to his lips. He said into
my hand, ''We must get married before I leave.''

I said, ''We must?''

''Well, yes.''

''Whatever for? Gresham, you have to leave tomorrow.
There really is no time to get married.''

''But I want you to know how much I love you.''

''I know.''

I laid my head on his chest. The hair tickled my cheek.
From my position, I could see into the sitting room. I caught
sight of the fruit bowl on the coffee table.

''Gresham?''

''Yes?''

''Are you hungry?''

He laughed. He rolled me off him, propped himself on
his elbow, and ran his finger along my cheek. ''Now that
you mention it, I am.''

''Would you like an apple?''

He looked where I was looking. ''That would be a good
start.'' He began to get up.

''No, stay there. I'll get you one.''

''No. Don't move.''

He was up and across the bedroom. I watched him walk.
I loved him. He called to me, ''Would you rather have an
orange?''

''Well . . .''

''You'll think of Miami Beach, Lily. All the nice things
you've told me about.''

I saw Johnny Q's face. I saw the Putty Man painting his

murals. I saw Eddie G shooting an arrow. I couldn't really answer.

"It's good to think about your old friends, Lily. Now, I know how much they must have loved you, too."

I watched him pick the biggest, fattest orange. He held it up for me to see. He made a cut into it with his teeth. As he walked back to the bed, he peeled it for me. I could see the juice squirting out and watched how intent Gresham was not to make a mess. He divided the orange into sections and held the pieces out to me.

"Lily, you're crying!"

He put the orange down on the night table on a Kleenex. He took me in his arms and said, "You could ask Rexhault to take you to Miami Beach on the way back to Tortuga. Don't cry."

"That's not why I'm crying. Thinking of Miami Beach gave me a nice feeling."

"Then what's wrong, Lily?"

"I'm crying because I do love you so. And I want that war to end soon. I want you to come back and marry me, and we'll have some little children."

"I will come back, and that is what we will do."

Gresham and I had breakfast with Rexhault. Charles would take Gresham to the train station. Gresham right away said, "Lily would like to ask something of you, Rexhault. She hesitates to ask, though."

"What would you like, Lily?"

I looked at Gresham. He'd taken the bull by the horns for me. Was I angry at that? No, I wasn't. I was grateful.

"Rexhault, before we go back to Tortuga, I would like to show Eddie G my medals."

Rexhault waited for a minute. Several times he started to say something but would stop. Then he said, "Your mother doesn't want you to think of her the way she used to be. She doesn't want you to remember."

"Well, that's very silly."

"I know. But for her it's not silliness, it's a fear. Her irrational fear of losing you."

"That's because she turned away from her mother, and then her mother upped and committed suicide. But Ma had to turn away. Her mother could have killed us, too. You know, Rexhault, I'm getting tired of pussyfooting around Ma. She won't know about my going there till I'm back, and she won't have to worry that I won't feel the same about her because she'll be able to see that I *do* feel the same about her, even though I've been back to Miami Beach."

Gresham smiled at me. Rexhault was still apprehensive. So I said, "I'll just have to go myself." Now, Rexhault raised his right eyebrow, Gresham his left. "Of course, Ma will never forgive you if you let me go alone."

They laughed. Rexhault settled himself back into his chair. "You couldn't go alone even if you wanted to. You would be recognized. It could be terrible."

"I'll dye my hair red."

Gresham smirked. Rexhault sighed. He said, "Lily, I want you to know about a great writer, Thomas Wolfe. He said—"

"Rexhault, you are talking to a Yale man," I told him. "I know what Mr. Wolfe said. But you can't go home again only if you're looking to find things just as they were. All I want is to talk to my coach again and go for a nice beach walk with Johnny Q. And I'm dying to see what the Putty Man's painted since I left."

Gresham said, "Who?"

"A Negro man who fixes windows. But he's a great artist. He painted murals on all the new hotels. And he used to take care of me sometimes when Johnny Q was busy. Oh, Gresham, you should see the Putty Man's murals. And you will someday. After the war, we'll go have a honeymoon at Miami Beach, and I will show them to you." I looked at Rexhault. "So what do you say?"

Rexhault said, "Don't dye your hair. We'll go."

Saying good-bye to Gresham wasn't so bad, because he and I were prepared and we were fortified by love. Gresham said he would do everything he could to get away to see me before his assignment. It was Rexhault, actually, who had a hard time saying good-bye. He felt very bad. When he shook Gresham's hand, he gripped it hard and held on to Gresham's elbow with his other hand. He told Gresham to be careful, as all fathers do with their sons. Gresham liked having to say good-bye to Rexhault, I could tell.

I said, "Good-bye, Gresham."

He said, "Good-bye, Lily."

It was sweet sorrow for sure.

The car pulled away. Rexhault said, "There is a fine young man."

"Yes. That's what he is."

"Very brave."

"Rexhault?"

"Hmmm . . ."

"Stop."

He looked into my face. "Forgive me, Lily."

"I'm worried about him, too."

"I know. I'm sorry, Lily."

"Will we take your private Pullman to Florida?"

"Yes, my dear, we will be in our Pullman, but it will be full of soldiers right along with us."

"Then that should be fun."

"Yes, it should."

"When will we leave?"

"Tomorrow."

"I would like to see the *Normandie* once more, before we go. I want to see that she really did go down, so I won't make believe she didn't."

"I understand. We will go there now."

The ship was good and dead. The black smoke had been cleared off by a cold wind. She lay on her side, and it was as if the Loch Ness monster had died and washed up on-shore.

There was a great feeling of shame hanging over the sight. The ship's underside with all her propellers and screws and bare metal was a gruesome sight exposed that way. It was worse than gruesome. I thought that all the people standing around staring at her underbelly was a terrible thing. A heartbreaking thing.

Rexhault said to me, ''What we must not forget, Lily, in our grief, is that there are other ships in the Hawaiian waters that look like this, and they are filled with thousands of sailors. And there are many more sailors badly burned and injured. There was no loss of life here.''

''No.''

I imagined the *Normandie* submerged completely and full of sailors who all looked like the Whiffenpoofs and like Gresham's divers.

''Rexhault, I don't know how people can do things to other people that the human mind is barely able to picture. I can't imagine dropping bombs on people.''

''Many people can imagine just such things, and I'm afraid they like what they see.''

''I want to go.''

He took my arm. Charles was back. He was still staring at the *Normandie* even as he pulled away. He had tears in his eyes, Charles did.

Chapter 20

Mr. Thomas Wolfe and my mother knew what they were talking about. Miami Beach belonged to the military. All the hotels were now confiscated, and soldiers practiced killing each other on the sand.

The combination of war games and soldiers who spent all their free time getting drunk led to loads of broken windows. The Putty Man had a lot of work.

The Putty Man was an extraordinary man. All his murals were being painted over. He said to me, "Well, I know for a fact that my pictures are right where I left them—just that they're hidin' under a layer of cheap paint. Long as I know they're still on the walls, I am satisfied."

I told him that after the war, when Miami Beach was back to normal, I'd see to it that they would all be restored. He said, laughing, "And no one will be able to stop you, child."

We brought Rexhault to the Lincoln Theatre, which the army wasn't interested in turning into anything, and Rexhault was taken aback by the Putty Man's artwork—the naked ladies under the African trees. Rexhault asked the Putty Man to come with us to Loggerhead Key and paint a mural behind the bar of the Radar Room.

The Putty Man said he'd try to come out there as soon as he could do the job, but that he would take no pay, only his meals and a place to sleep. That way he could feel free to paint as he saw fit and would not be obligated to make what

anyone else saw as fit, meaning Rexhault. Rexhault liked
that. The Putty Man agreed to come, but not with us on
Rexhault's yacht. He said he had to spend what time there
was left to spend with his sons. "See," he said, "I'm a
family man first, an artist second, and a putty man third."
Rexhault and the Putty Man shook hands.

The Putty Man told me that Johnny Q was at Vero Beach,
hired by the Boston Braves to work on building up a new
spring-training camp with all the latest paraphernalia. The
Putty Man said it was a mighty big project, and Johnny Q
would be a pitching coach once it was ready for all the
ballplayers who had gone off to war. I wondered about
Johnny Q taking on such a project all by himself. I asked if
Eddie G was helping him on it, and the Putty Man said no,
that Eddie G had moved on, he didn't know where to.

On the way to Vero Beach, we drove past an air-force
flying school. All the air-force men were Negro. The U.S.
government had decided to let Negro men fly airplanes.

I said, "Could we just stop here, Rexhault? I want to
inquire about my friend who was on our Olympic team."

"Certainly, Lily. Charles."

Archie Williams was there. I told his commanding officer
to please tell Lieutenant Williams that the albino Negro diver
from Berlin wished to see him. Through the window, I saw
him running across the parade grounds showing the same
great form he demonstrated to Mr. Adolf Hitler when he
won his gold medal.

Framed in the doorway, he grinned, saluted his superior,
and said, "Lily, welcome to Spookwaffe!"

While Rexhault had lunch with a general, Archie and his
instructor flew me and Charles (I knew Charles would want
to) through the air in a B-52 bomber. Flying was as exhil-
arating as Archie had promised. He said he finally knew
what it was like to do what I had done all my life. Then he
told his instructor to try an inward pike. The plane started
to roll, and I shouted, "No, no!" How Archie laughed.

When our trip to Vero Beach continued, my nervousness
about seeing Johnny Q again had drained right out my toes.

It was a good thing. My calm allowed me to be tough while Johnny Q fell apart.

I saw him before he saw me. He looked stronger and much younger than how I remembered him. His hair was still gray, but it was combed. He was off the sauce. I called to him and went running. He bawled like a baby, and once we were through hugging, we both began to blabber at once.

"I am so proud," he said.

"If they gave gold medals for fastballs, Johnny Q, you'd have a million of them."

He showed us his camp. He was very pleased with the work he'd done, laying the whole thing out and putting schedules down on paper. The grass on the playing field was emerald green and fine as moss. It would have to wait, though, but not too long, we hoped. Johnny Q got two mitts, and we had a good catch, though I was a little rusty at first.

He told me that I should open a camp of my own for divers, and for swimmers, too, seeing as how just divers wouldn't be enough for such an operation. He felt that talented kids who hadn't a good facility available to them should be able to at least visit one for the months before the Olympic Games.

Rexhault said, "What a splendid idea. And we certainly have the start of such a facility available."

I said, "We do?"

He said, "The Normandie."

"Oh, sure, Rexhault. The Radar Room would be such a swell influence on the athletes."

"Actually . . ." He coughed. I'd never heard a nervous cough come out of Rexhault.

"Actually, what?"

"Your mother and I have noticed that the action seems to be moving to Havana."

Havana. They were leaving Loggerhead Key. Following the action. Action could mean just about anything. Before all that could really sink in and allow me to speak, Rexhault continued.

"We expected, of course, to take you with us, or suggest that you go to a university to get a legitimate degree. We intended to discuss the situation with you as soon as you and I returned to the Normandie. But now I realize, Lily, that you could stay on Loggerhead Key, if you like, because the hotel is yours. The key is yours. It's in your name.''

"It is?''

"Yes.''

"I've never owned anything before.''

"You do now—compliments of Jean Laffite.''

"Ha!''

"Really, Lily, it is something to talk over with Johnny Q.''
I said, "I'd need Eddie G. Where is he?''

Johnny Q told me that Eddie G was an assistant coach at UCLA. He'd been recruited when I went to New York.

I said, "But that's so wonderful! He must be teaching those California kids so much.''

"Well, he's there because of you. And I'm here because I thought someday you just might want to come back to Florida and see your old pal Johnny Q, and I didn't want you to find me skunked, layin' under a palm tree wettin' my pants.''

After he said that, Rexhault and I had to spend a few minutes calming Johnny Q down, and then I told Johnny Q I had a friend named Dr. Gallileo who he'd really get on with, because he was quite a weeper, too. That led to my telling all about my adventures finding out the story of my granny maybe being the daughter-in-law of Jean Laffite and about Rum Keg, too. Johnny Q told me that such an adventure was a real knee-slapper. And that led to him giving me a rundown on all the Fraley kids and how Mr. and Mrs. Fraley were in California, too.

Before we had to leave, I invited Johnny Q to come visit me at "my" hotel whenever he felt like it. I got Eddie G's address and number, for he was about to be recruited again. At least I would have somebody to talk to about an Olympic training camp.

On Rexhault's yacht, I wrote a long, long letter to Gresham, full of love and news and plans for what I would do with the Normandie and would he be able to call it home, too?

When Rexhault and my mother left for Havana six months later, I was on my own. The first thing I did was to pack up and go see Eddie G and tell him all about the Olympic swimming facility I was planning. He told me he was best at coaching individuals, not teams. I told him that would be just fine. When Gresham came back, he and I and Gresham would combine what we each did best, and our athletes would have a little of everything. I would shoot movies, I told him, the way Mr. Modeen did. He said, "You going to offer Modeen a job, too?"

Right away, I said, "Nope." Then we both laughed. And I said, "Well, maybe." Eddie G told me he'd be waiting on my call.

The second thing I did on my own was to go to a funeral in Philadelphia for one of the Gresham's divers. He'd been hit by mortar fire. He was a nice boy.

My mother called me from Cuba when I got back to the Normandie. She was very upset because she knew that not only had I been to the funeral, but that I still hadn't once heard from Gresham Young. So my mother told me that if Gresham never came back, just having a memory of Gresham was more than what most people had. And she told me that there were a lot of other missing men in the world searching for a port. She was right about all that, too.

In 1944, when I saw *Winged Victory* and listened to Fred Waring's band playing a jazzy version of "We Are Poor Little Lambs" in the middle of the movie, I still knew that though my mother was right about so much, she was wrong to think that Gresham might not come back. He would. He surely would.

About the Author

Mary-Ann Tirone Smith is the author of the widely acclaimed THE BOOK OF PHOEBE and LAMENT FOR A SILVER-EYED WOMAN. She spent two years in Cameroon with the Peace Corps after getting her B.A. from Central Connecticut State University. She lives with her husband and two children in Ridgefield, Connecticut.